"I was trying not to wake you."

Emma glanced over her shoulder. "Figured you could use the sleep."

Gage joined her in the kitchen, rubbing the sleep from his eyes. "I didn't even hear him until just now. Sorry."

"You were out cold." Emma finished shaking the bottle, then cradled the baby. "Go to bed, Gage. I've got him. You're exhausted. Let me do this."

His eyes pricked with a strange sensation. The woman was selfless. Emma watched out for him in a way that he wasn't sure he'd ever experienced before outside his family. She made him want...a future. A wife. A family.

Her.

All things that he wasn't sure he had enough faith to try again.

Frustration bubbled up. Why had Emma come into his life now? When it was too late?

Which was why he *had* to stop thinking of her as he'd begun to: his saving grace, his new beginning. Because she was none of those things for him. Not if he truly cared about her. Not if he wanted her to have the future she deserved.

Jill Lynn is a member of American Christian Fiction Writers and won the ACFW Genesis Contest in 2013. She has a bachelor's degree in communications from Bethel University. A native of Minnesota, Jill now lives in Colorado with her husband and two children. She's an avid reader of happily-ever-afters and a fan of grace, laughter and thrift stores. Connect with her at jill-lynn.com.

Books by Jill Lynn

Love Inspired

Colorado Grooms

Visit the Author Profile page at Harlequin.com for more titles.

The Rancher's Unexpected Baby

Jill Lynn

HARLEQUIN® LOVE INSPIRED®

Recycling programs for this product may not exist in your area.

LOVE INSPIRED BOOKS

ISBN-13: 978-1-335-47897-9

The Rancher's Unexpected Baby

Copyright © 2019 by Jill Buteyn

www.Harlequin.com

Printed in U.S.A.

A new commandment I give unto you,
that ye love one another; as I have loved you,
that ye also love one another.
—*John* 13:34

For my dad—I'm so thankful for your wisdom, your sense of humor and that you taught us about Jesus. So many lives have been touched because of your gift of sharing the gospel.

Chapter One

I'm not a stalker, Emma Wilder assured herself while attempting to peer inconspicuously out the front windows of Len's grocery store. Gage Frasier's Jeep Grand Cherokee was parked in the first spot, so it would be almost impossible for her not to notice him as he sat behind his steering wheel. His face was as haggard as a mom waiting at her child's hospital bedside.

Something—or someone—had upset her brother's friend.

The hand pressing the phone to his ear stayed put while the other clutched the steering wheel in a death grip. Squeeze. Release. Squeeze—

"Need anything else, dear?" The clerk, Dolores, held out Emma's two bags.

"No, thanks. Say hi to that cutie granddaughter of yours for me." Emma snagged the reusable canvas totes and headed for the exit.

I'm also not a meddler, Emma reminded herself as she stepped outside into the freezer currently known as Colorado. She would walk right by Gage without stopping to check if he was okay. Or figure out what had him so distressed.

Her Mini Cooper was two spots past his vehicle. It had been an impulse buy from the small used-car lot in town. Done *without* her big brother's approval. That right there made the purchase worthwhile. Even though the little thing might not be built for crashing through snowdrifts, it had handled perfectly well so far…in the three weeks she'd had it. Never mind that no major snow had fallen in that span of time.

Brr! The ice-cold air pierced her lungs, and her organs complained like unruly children. When she was just steps from Gage's vehicle, his free arm jutted into the air in a move similar to one her friend's boys would do while pretending to be ninjas. What could have Gage so distraught? The man was usually so…*Gage*. Calm. A bit stoic at times. Definitely not one to be playing ninja without good reason.

And his poor forehead—all of those worry lines. If he were a woman, he'd need to run home and apply a mask of some sort to thwart the wrinkles that would sprout at the first opportunity.

Phone pressed to his left ear, Gage motioned to her… as if she should open the passenger door of his Jeep. Because she was standing right next to the window, peering in like the stalker she'd just claimed not to be.

Emma couldn't walk past a baby, a puppy or, it seemed, a Gage. Anyone in need beckoned to her like pickles to a pregnant mama. Or so she'd heard.

She waved, as if to say…what? *Don't mind me. I'm just standing here staring at you?* Again Gage signaled for her to open the door. He probably thought there was something wrong with her car. Or her. It was all of two degrees outside, and she was shivering next to his vehicle like a frozen statue about to break into ice chips. Too late to run for it now or explain herself—somehow—and escape, since Gage was still on the phone. So she opened the door and got in. Shut it behind her.

If only she had superpowers and could make herself invisible. Or shrink down to penny size.

Emma inhaled, fighting to keep it discreet when what she really wanted to do was gulp in the men's cologne section scent that permeated Gage's vehicle. One of the many romance novels she consumed on a weekly basis would probably describe it as sandalwood or citrus or cedar, but Emma would label it *yum*.

His caramel voice filled the car. "I understand. Yes. I see." He reached over, midsentence, and cranked the heat. The fact that he was obviously discussing a dire circumstance on the phone and would still do a small gesture like that warmed her. Literally. Gage, despite all of his inner turmoil, was still chivalrous. Kind. Droolworthy.

"I'll get back to you. Thank you." He pressed the end-call button.

Time to scram. Obviously Gage had a lot on his plate. Emma gripped the door handle. "Thanks for the warmup. My car is only a few over, so I'll just…"

Gage was lost somewhere, his eyes glazed. Maybe even a tremble in his strong chin. *What in the world?*

"Gage?" Her hand dropped back to her lap, shoulders twisting to face him. She gained his empty stare. "What happened? Are you okay?"

"No." His head shook with a vengeance. "Not even a little bit."

Emma waited. She'd become good at it over the years.

Being the younger sister of twin siblings who were strong and competitive often left her dead last. And they all ran a guest ranch together, so she'd had lots of practice learning to be patient. For the most part, Emma was content with her role. God must have made her that way, because she didn't remember wanting too much more than the life she had. Except for one small problem. She was a romantic in a town that didn't allow for that. The men in Westbend were few and far between. Too old. Too young. Not attracted to her or the other way around. And when one did pay attention to her and garner her interest… Well, she knew from experience that led to trouble.

"That sounded like a tough phone call. If you don't want to talk about it, I under—"

"Do you remember my friend Zeke who passed away about two weeks ago?"

"Yes. Of course." A young father who'd been flying himself from Aspen to Denver when his plane had crashed *and* had already lost his wife. It was all so tragic. How could Emma forget? Gage had been a mess. In shock.

"His nine-month-old son—Hudson."

Emma waited while Gage stared at the dash. Finally his eyes landed on her. "Zeke named me as his guardian."

Now it was her turn to enter the stages of shock. She didn't say anything right away. Just let that gigantic news simmer. "Did you know he had?"

Gage's shoulders inched up. "After Leila died, he was such a mess. His grief was so intense. He asked me to take care of Hudson if anything ever happened to him. Of course I said yes in that moment. I'd wanted to do anything to ease his turmoil. To help. But I didn't know he'd gone and made it legal." His hands scrubbed through his hair, leaving the normally well behaved deep-brown, almost-black locks in disarray. "I'm the absolute worst person for this. I don't even want to have kids."

Emma couldn't be further from Gage in that regard. She craved a house full of little ones. Someday. She was only twenty-three and in no rush. But definitely someday.

"That doesn't mean you can't do it." Emma had full confidence in that, even if Gage didn't.

"That's exactly what it means." Gage's weariness expanded, slithering across the console.

"So what happens now?"

"That was Zeke's aunt. She's keeping Hudson for now and his nanny is helping out still, but it's not a long-term solution. His aunt Rita has too many health issues. I told her I needed some time to process. She understood. I asked her to check with the other family members and see if there's anyone else interested in keeping the baby. She's going to talk with her husband—he's named as the executor of the will—and they'll investigate some other options." His groan reeked of desperation. "Anywhere is better than with me. A single twenty-nine-year-old guy? That's crazy. What was Zeke thinking?"

That you'd be perfect. That maybe a baby would heal that big ol' hole inside your chest that Nicole carved. Gage's ex-wife had certainly done a number on him.

"And what if there's not someone else to take him?"

Gage dropped his phone into the cup holder, and it clattered with the unusually careless movement. "Then I'll deal with that then. In the meantime, I'm just going to pray there is."

"I'll pray, too." Except… Emma wasn't so sure she agreed with Gage's petition for another home for Hudson. She'd pray hard for that sweet baby. That God would provide a loving family for him. That he'd end up exactly where he was supposed to.

And if the answer to those requests was the man sitting next to her in the driver's seat, then she'd ask that Gage would accept that, too.

Three days later, Gage pounded on the front door of Luc Wilder's cabin. He usually didn't show up unannounced, especially now that Luc had married Cate. But desperate times and all of that.

When no one answered, he knocked again. He needed…someone. He had to process all of this Hudson stuff with a friend, and Luc fit that bill.

The door wrenched open as a swirl of frigid wind wrapped around him. Remnants of a dusting of snow blew from the roof and wafted behind the collar of his wool jacket. His coat blocked most of the chill, but a Mount Everest parka wouldn't be enough to handle the cold snap that had been hanging on for the last week.

Emma stood inside, her questioning look likely matching his. Why was she answering Luc's door? She must be over visiting Cate. The two of them had become good friends since Cate had shown up at the Wilder Ranch with a young daughter Luc never knew he had.

Wearing a long sweater and leggings with fuzzy socks, Emma looked like she'd just crawled out from under a cozy blanket. Her hair was up in a haphazard bun, her face devoid of makeup.

No blame for his chilly intrusion registered. Emma didn't really get upset, did she? At least Gage had never been the recipient of her anger.

"Hey, Emma. Is Luc here?"

"No, we finished up moving the last of our things yesterday. He and Cate are living at the house now, and Mackenzie and I are here."

That's right. How had he forgotten? Luc and Cate were expecting twins next summer, so they'd planned to move into the four-bedroom house that Emma and her sister Mackenzie had occupied, and the girls planned to switch over to the two-bedroom cabin that had been Luc's. Guess they already had.

The last few days since he'd found out about being named Hudson's guardian, Gage had functioned in a blur.

"I completely forgot about the move. I'll check there. Thanks." He stepped back, his vision already directed toward the house down the hill.

"Wait," Emma called out. "Luc's not there. He, Cate and Ruby are running some errands, and Mackenzie's not home, either, so it's just me." Another draft of piercing air whipped around them. "Can you come in? Please? It's freezing out there."

When he didn't move fast enough, Emma stepped outside in her socks, grabbed his arm and tugged him into the cabin. The door clicked shut behind him, hemming in the warmth.

A fire crackled, orange flames licking the dried wood. Emma steered him to the couch across from it and gave him a gentle shove so that he landed on the cushion.

"I'm going to make us some tea."

Gage removed his jacket, tossing it over the back of the couch as Emma bustled along the small line of cabinets and appliances at the front of the cabin. She filled a kettle with water and placed it on the burner. After removing two mugs from the cupboard, she opened a cabinet and retrieved a wooden box.

"Chamomile okay?"

Gage had never had a cup of tea in his life, so... "Sure."

"Honey or lemon or milk with it?"

"No, thanks." At least that was his guess. He liked his coffee black, so maybe tea fell into the same category.

When the whistle blew, she poured the steaming liquid into the mugs, added tea bags and brought them into the living room. The cup she set before him on the coffee table said *breathe* in scrawling letters. Was she sending him a message?

Emma sat in the chair that flanked the couch, one leg tucked beneath her. "Okay, what's going on? Is it the stuff with the baby? Hudson?"

He nodded.

"I've been praying about him so much. Luc and Cate have been, too. I know you'd rather have my brother for a sounding board, but currently I'm all you've got. So, spill. I'll listen."

Maybe Emma would have some good advice. She was in charge of the Kids' Club at the ranch and had a definite gift for dealing with children. Or maybe she'd offer to keep the baby herself.

And if she could hear his horrible thoughts, she'd be mortified.

It wasn't that Gage didn't want to honor his friend's request or even that he didn't want Hudson. But he was nowhere near the right person for taking care of a baby or raising a child. Not in the least.

"I talked to Zeke's aunt Rita again today. There isn't another family member who can take him. Rita's in her late sixties, and she and her husband have some health problems, so they're not an option. There is no one. That's why Zeke left him to me in the first place. I thought he'd just been delirious with grief." Gage picked up his mug and took a sip. The tea had an apple-like flavor. Not terrible. Not the best thing he'd ever tasted. At least it added some moisture to his parched mouth. "But I guess not. I asked the nanny if she could watch Hudson at the ranch, but she's already accepted a new position that starts next week. She was apologetic. Said she needs the money and took the other job because she hadn't known what the future held with Hudson. And, of course, the new family is counting on her now, so she's out. I should have talked to her right away. Asked her to stay on." But he'd been certain there would be another family member or couple who would be a better fit for Hudson. Gage had never imagined he'd end up actually keeping the boy.

Emma twisted the mug in her hands back and forth. "You still don't feel…qualified to be his guardian?"

"Not in the least."

"What happens if you say no? Can you even say no?"

"I can ask the court to be relieved of the guardianship."

"Then what?"

Gage set his mug on the coffee table, his next words weighing down his tongue. "I think he'd go into the foster care system."

Emma's features warred between disbelief and dismay. "But you wouldn't let that happen, right? I mean, you have to take him." Her lips formed a tight bud. "I'm sorry. I've said too much, I just—"

"You're right. I do have to. At least for the time being."

Gage would honor what he'd told Zeke. He would take care of Hudson—by keeping him temporarily while searching until he found a better situation for the boy.

Emma relaxed visibly, color returning to her cheeks.

"But I still don't think I'm the right person for this. I have no idea how to take care of a baby. I know absolutely nothing. What am I supposed to do?"

He met her steel-blue eyes, letting the questions brim. Emma was twenty-three. Six years younger than him. His friend's little sister. And yet here he was dumping all of this on her and expecting answers. But she was good that way. The kind of comforting person everyone wanted to be around.

From the moment she'd tugged him inside, a little of the burden crushing him had ebbed. The Emma Effect.

She brightened. "I'll help." She set her tea on the coffee table with excited force, moving to the edge of her seat. "This is our slow season. We only have a few church groups here and there on the weekends. Maybe a corporate event. I can work around those, and, truthfully, they don't even need me because there's usually no Kids' Club. I can watch Hudson while you get things in order."

Steel drums pounded inside his skull. Emma's idea could work. It was asking a lot of her, but Gage could pay her. Since his uncle had left him the ranch free and clear, it had allowed Gage to take some risks that had paid off. The ranch had done well for him. Plus, Zeke— being himself and completely prepared—had left provisions for taking care of Hudson.

"If you're serious, that might just work. You watching him would buy me the time to find a better home for him."

"Or—" Emma's hand lifted in an endearing I-just-thought-of-this gesture "—maybe *you* have the right home for him, and by having him stay with you, you'll figure that out."

"That's not the case, Emma. I am sure of that. I might feel differently if I ever planned or hoped to have kids one day, but I don't. Not everyone is built for having children."

Disappointment creased the corners of her arresting eyes. With her light brown hair and fresh complexion, Emma wasn't supermodel gorgeous. She was more... girl-next-door pretty. She was also innocent and sweet and crazy to think that he could or should raise Hudson.

"It would be a short-term fix. Maybe it's wrong. Maybe God will send fire and brimstone down on me for it, but I'm only going to take Hudson on a provisional basis. Please tell me you'll still help now that I've admitted that. Because I don't know what I'm going to do if you can't." Gage swallowed a frenzied laugh. "No pressure or anything."

Emma took a sip of tea, the lower curve of her lip partially hidden behind the mug rim. "I'm the one who offered. I'm not going to renege. It's all going to work out, Gage."

"Anyone ever tell you that your optimism knows no bounds?"

She laughed, a happy, infectious sound. "I *know* you can do this."

And Gage knew this—Emma might be full of fanciful ideas, but he was not. A more fitting home existed for Hudson. He just had to find it.

If someone handed Emma a baby, she'd tuck the bundle against her stomach like a football and run for it so no one could take the child back. Gage couldn't sprint fast enough in the other direction. He was a single twenty-nine-year-old guy. Of course caring for a baby wasn't at the top of his wish list, but God must have put this exact thing in Gage's life for a reason.

Usually the man across from her was all things strong and put together. But tonight he wore his confusion and weariness much like his navy blue sweater, jeans and brown lace-up boots.

When she'd opened the door, he'd looked as lost as he had in his vehicle the other day.

Emma took a sip from her vintage Rocky Mountain National Park mug that had been in her parents' cupboard for as long as she could remember, the tea's subtle undertones familiar and soothing. When her parents had purged and moved out of state, she hadn't been able to let the childhood memory go. Along with a few others.

"We'll figure it out, Gage. You're not alone in this. Might feel like it, but you have people willing to help. You have a tribe over here. We're not going to leave you hanging."

The faintest smile touched his mouth. "Thanks. I appreciate that. It's just…usually I know exactly what needs to be done, and I just…do it." He reached for his tea, downing a swig as if the liquid could right all that had gone topsy-turvy in his life. "But this…"

But this time, he knew what he *should* do and he was fighting it. Emma got that. She had a little feistiness in her, too. Not as much as her sister, Mackenzie, but still. It was almost never easy to do the right thing. The thing God was asking for that was too big, too hard.

But she also believed Zeke must have had a reason for choosing Gage as the baby's guardian.

She'd help Gage with Hudson because she wanted to. Because it only made sense for her to lend a hand. But she didn't plan to admit to Gage that she had ulterior motives. She believed this baby could heal something in him that his ex-wife had broken.

Gage might view himself as a temporary guardian for Hudson, but if Emma had anything to say about it, this situation would be permanent.

Chapter Two

Gage strode out of Rita's house on Friday morning with Hudson strapped into a mobile car seat. He half expected the police to show up with guns blazing and accuse him of baby stealing.

Since he'd said yes to assuming temporary guardianship, things had progressed quickly. The past three days, he'd visited Hudson at Rita's to get better acquainted with him.

Gage had known the boy since birth, but during recent months he'd only seen Zeke a handful of times and the baby twice.

Thankfully, the ranch foreman who had worked for Gage's uncle had stayed after his passing. Along with the other cowboys, Ford had been covering for Gage's absence this week. The man had given Gage a crash course in cattle ranching over the last two years. Without his coaching, Gage would have failed a thousand times over.

Thankfully Emma had also agreed to help him out today by coming with him to pick up Hudson. When he'd asked her to consider accompanying him, she'd answered, "What's there to think about? Of course I will."

Her giving heart made his resemble a lump of coal.

They'd already loaded the car with piles of Hudson's things. Toys. Clothes. Gage had baby equipment he wouldn't have a clue what to do with up to his ears and mashed against the windows of his Grand Cherokee.

He couldn't believe he was doing this. Taking a baby home with him. But his name was on the paperwork, so here they went.

You'd think with how much he'd loved Zeke, this would be second nature for Gage. He should be saying things like, *Of course I'll take the baby. This is what Zeke chose and I want to honor my friend.* But their friendship didn't mean he was the right person for this.

Which made him wonder why he'd said yes when Zeke had asked him to take care of Hudson. It had been shortly after Leila had passed away from complications from childbirth. Sounded medieval, but it still happened on rare occasions. Zeke had been a mess. Obviously with good reason. Gage had simply been trying to reassure him, never thinking that one day a casual promise would turn into this. Never thinking that Zeke would be killed in a plane crash when his son was just nine months old.

Now, not only was he grieving the loss of his friend, he was supposed to fill his shoes in his son's life? And how, exactly, would he do that?

At least he had help in the form of the cheerful, capable woman currently opening the back door of his vehicle.

Gage slid the car seat in, and Emma climbed in after, securing it while he went around to the driver's side.

After some adjustments—making sure the seat was snug, removing their jackets for the drive and buckling themselves in—they were on the road. Emma sat in the back seat with Hudson, talking to him in that soothing tone of hers until he cooed back at her.

A few miles later, Emma announced that Hudson had fallen asleep.

"Good." Nap time Gage could handle.

"It's going to be okay, Gage. I promise this is all going to work out."

He met her bright eyes in the rearview mirror. "You can't promise that, Emma."

"It's not a *me* promise, it's a God one. He works things together for good. Even the kind of mountains that don't appear climbable."

Gage wanted to tell her that Hudson wasn't a mountain and ask if she could turn down her optimism for the day so he could just stay worried and distraught. But asking Emma not to be positive and hopeful would be like requesting she forgo the use of her limbs. It was as much a part of her as the blood pumping through her veins.

"I know this isn't what you wanted for Hudson. And that you plan to find another, *better*—" Emma's version of polite sarcasm laced the last word "—home for him, but in the meantime, while you're keeping him, you need to want him, even if it's only temporary. It's important. Especially with how he's being uprooted. Babies can sense more than we realize, and he'll know if you're only halfway in. So at least be committed for the time you have him. Please."

"I don't know what I'm doing." Gage said it more for himself than in answer to Emma.

"You don't have to. Just love him. The rest is gravy."

Gravy. Emma made it sound so easy when it would be anything but. His hands strangled the steering wheel, then loosened. But Emma was right. Gage had been raised in a fantastic home with parents who thought he hung the moon. It did matter what Hudson felt over the next few days or weeks or however long this situation lasted until they found a more suitable family for him.

"You can do this, Gage." Did Emma have a cheerleading background he'd somehow missed hearing about? Did the woman hoard pom-poms in her closet? She was full of confidence in him that was undeserved. He'd already botched a marriage and could so quickly and easily mess things up with Hudson.

"Did I say too much?" The mirror framed Emma's face as it contorted with concern.

"No. I needed to hear it. Thanks."

She beamed in answer, and her attractiveness ramped up to a level that caught Gage by surprise. Her lightest-shade-of-brown hair was up in a ponytail today, and she wore skinny jeans, Converse shoes, and a charcoal sweater with a jumbo-sized white heart on the front. Emma had a simplicity about her. An even-keeled nature. She reminded him of…homemade chocolate chip cookies right out of the oven. That's the kind of comfort she offered.

"Thanks for coming with me today. It was over and above."

"You're welcome. There's nowhere else I'd rather be than with this cutie." Emma's mouth softened as her gaze rested on Hudson.

God had worked today out, that was for sure. Gage would give Him all of the credit for the woman in the back seat currently making everything better for every passenger in the car.

When they arrived at his house, vehicles belonging to Luc and his twin sister, Mackenzie, were parked out front beside Emma's car. Gage twisted, meeting Emma's not-so-innocent look. "Any chance you had something to do with this?"

"What? Me? Never." The suppressed chuckle that followed contradicted her words. She couldn't lie to save her life. A good quality in Gage's book.

The front door of the house opened and the group exited as he parked and cut the Jeep's engine—so much for giving Luc a key in case of emergency.

Luc stayed to help unload the car while his wife, Cate, their four-year-old daughter Ruby, Emma and Mackenzie focused on getting the car seat with a still-sleeping Hudson inside. Gage doubted it took four females to transport the boy, but he didn't mind the reprieve.

In true Colorado nature, the weather had changed yesterday, swinging from freezing to a pleasant fifty degrees. With the heat from the sun, the day felt balmy.

"So," Luc slapped him on the back, "how you holding up?"

Gage opened the back hatch, amazed everything didn't tumble out. "Okay. I guess. Think I'm in shock. I only found out about being named Hudson's guardian a week ago. Still haven't wrapped my mind around it."

"Understandable." Luc snagged a saucer that had various stations of activity around the top. "I can't say I totally get what you're feeling, but then again…"

True. Luc hadn't found out Ruby existed until last summer. So his friend got the surprise part in all of this. And probably the feeling-inept portion, too.

Gage scooped up a box labeled Toys. "How am I supposed to do this?"

"Not sure. Wish I had answers for you."

"Emma seems to think if I close my eyes and make

a wish, unicorns and rainbows will appear and all will be well."

Luc laughed. "She's probably expecting this to turn out like one of those romantic books or movies she's hooked on. We have cable just so she can stream the Hallmark Channel."

"I would make a good leading man."

A snort from Luc followed his quip.

The next few minutes unloading with Luc felt like a sliver of normal. The smell of the ranch—a mixture of hay and dirt since the cattle were over the hill—brought Gage's shoulders down about ten notches.

When he'd quit the law firm and moved out here with Nicole hoping to save their marriage, he hadn't expected to fall for ranching. But it suited him. He liked the physical labor. Being outdoors. Managing staff and cattle. The business side of things.

It was a surprisingly good fit. Not that he didn't enjoy practicing law. He still helped people out when the opportunity arose and picked up some contract work from his old firm when it fit his schedule. But the switch in lifestyle had been a godsend at a time when he'd needed it, and now he couldn't imagine going back to that fast-paced, cutthroat world.

Once they grabbed the last load, including a diaper bag that was thankfully a manly black backpack, the two of them tromped inside.

The kitchen had been taken over by women, a sight that had never happened in this house. In the short time Nicole had actually lived here before taking off, she'd only prepared a handful of meals. Cooking hadn't really been her thing. Having an affair a second time had been more up her alley.

The kitchen opened to the living room, a butcher-block island separating the spaces. It was covered with lunch items—a tray of meat and cheese and other sandwich toppings. Hudson had awakened and was now sitting in the high chair that someone had assembled. Ruby stood in front of him, entertaining. She wore a blue dress and red cowboy boots, her hair secured in two buns. Luc's daughter definitely had the inside demeanor to match her outside cuteness.

"We're going to be friends, okay? I thought we were going to be cousins, but Mommy said we weren't." Ruby leaned toward Hudson, voice dropping to a whisper that could be heard for miles. "But we can pretend."

Hudson chortled in response, filled with nothing less than adoration for the delightful girl in front of him.

"And we're going to ride horses, and we're going to get lots of treats from Mr. Joe." Apparently Joe—the Wilder Ranch head chef who was known for whipping up mouthwatering desserts—had gained a super fan in Ruby. The girl continued her initiation for the baby, listing all of the fun things she planned for them to do.

When Gage had attempted to picture this day, he hadn't imagined that it would turn out like this. These people filling the space. Hudson happy and not in tears at being torn first from his dad and then his nanny.

At least today—so far—had gone okay. If only Gage could confidently say the same thing about tomorrow.

Emma held Hudson with his head tucked against her shoulder as she paced the living room in Gage's house. The baby didn't like to be cradled sideways. She'd tried that already and had been informed by squirming and tears that Hudson did *not* appreciate the position. So upright it was.

It had been a long day. They'd left to get Hudson at eight this morning, and now it was thirteen hours later. The full house from earlier had dispersed, leaving only her, Gage and the baby. The man reminded Emma of a caged animal tonight. Trapped. Unable to sit still. He kept popping up to do things. He'd been out to the barn twice already even though his ranch hands knew what he was up against and had things covered.

Gage might not know what to do with himself, but he was going to have to figure that out—and quickly— because Emma was about to go home for the night. And the man who hadn't so much as held Hudson all day was about to be on his own.

No time like the present. She crossed to the kitchen where Gage was unloading the dishwasher. She hated to interrupt his task—because how attractive was a guy cleaning?—but she forced herself to. "Here you go." She deposited a drowsy Hudson in his arms despite his startled grunt of protest. "He should be ready to sleep. I think the late nap this afternoon messed up his schedule, but I've got him settled down."

Gage looked at the baby, then her, panic evident. "Maybe you should put him to bed before you go? He's already so comfortable with you."

Nice try, Counselor.

"I think it's better if you do it."

"Right now? But what do I…do?"

"Hold him." She pressed down on a grin. "I have to use the restroom. Be right back." She took her time inside the hallway bathroom, lollygagging, giving Gage time to adjust. When she returned, Hudson had started to fuss a bit. A drowsy, agitated complaint here and there.

Her fingers itched to take him back, but she resisted. Barely. "You're doing great. Just try to remain calm. He'll sense if you're not."

Gage's eyes shot to full moon size at that. The man had really great eyes. When he grinned, they crinkled at the corners, and the light sapphire contrasted with his dark hair, making the color pop.

"Now what?" He followed Emma to the front door.

"Now you both get some rest. I'll be back in the morning."

"Do I lay him in the portable crib?"

"Sure."

"Do you think he'll just…sleep?"

She hoped so.

"Are you sure you shouldn't just stay? I could sleep in the barn."

Emma laughed. Those were drastic measures to avoid a night with Hudson. And also very much like something she would read in one of her historical romance novels, with the man trying to save the woman's reputation from being tarnished.

"No need for that. You'll be fine." Her voice was bright. Phony to her own ears. "If you need anything or have a question—big or small—call me. I'll answer any time of the night." She kissed Hudson's forehead, silently praying that things would go well for him and Gage. "I'll see you two in the morning."

Crisp air nipped at her as she hurried to her car. The temperature had dropped dramatically once the sun had slipped behind the mountains. She got in, started the engine but then didn't budge.

Would Gage and Hudson be okay? What if the baby screamed all night? Should she be doing something more? Her windpipe shrunk down to straw proportions.

"God, I need You to handle this. Please." Emma couldn't fix this situation for any of them. And Gage had to step into his role as Hudson's caregiver. Emma would help him as much as she could, but the two of them needed to bond. If they formed an attachment, it would go yards toward Gage keeping Hudson. The kind of healing the man was unknowingly desperate for was currently in his arms in the shape of a wiggly baby boy.

Emma blasted the heat, then turned her phone up to the highest volume for texts or calls and switched off the other app notifications. If Gage needed her, she didn't want to miss him.

While she had her phone in hand, she sent a text to her sister-in-law, Cate. I'm doing the right thing leaving them, right? Guilt over abandoning Gage was piling up.

Thankfully Cate answered quickly.

Yes! If you stay, it will just prolong Gage figuring this out on his own. And, unfortunately, he has to. Zeke didn't name you as the baby's guardian. (Though had he known you, I have no doubt you'd have been number one on his list.) This is Gage's situation to handle. Come home.

Okay. You're right. Thanks.

Anytime. And if you happen to bring home a pizza, I won't complain. Kidding! Because I know you'd do exactly that. I already have heartburn and don't want to add to it.

Emma chuckled. Cate was eating for three, and she was doing an excellent job of it. And Luc was as doting as a husband could be. If Emma wasn't such a romantic, their relationship would be cause for mucho eye rolling. As it was, she was faintly envious of what they had. Luc and Cate had started off rocky, but once they'd figured out they were both still crazy about each other, they'd been solid. Steady.

Even with unexpected twins on the way.

The front light on Gage's house switched off. Was that a good sign? Was Hudson asleep? Why hadn't Emma thought to install some sort of video baby monitor? There was probably a kind that would have hooked up to an app on her phone. That would have been an excellent idea.

And completely intrusive.

Emma had claimed not to be a stalker, but based on her current thoughts, the accusation would definitely stick.

"Fine. I'll wait it out. Just for a bit." She switched off the engine. There was nothing wrong with sitting there for a little while just to make sure Gage or Hudson didn't panic. That way if Gage called or texted, she'd be close by to assist. If not, he didn't need to know she hadn't left yet. And she wasn't about to text Cate and relay her new plan, because she was pretty sure it wouldn't be met with approval.

Emma found a sweatshirt in the back that she could scrunch up as a pillow, reclined her seat and closed her eyes. After a short nap, she'd head home and no one would be the wiser.

She'd left him. Emma had promised to help, and now Gage was alone with a baby. He didn't even know how to change a diaper! Should he set an alarm for that sort of thing? Or would Hudson let him know when it was time? Wasn't there something about the diaper—or a line on it—changing color? Emma had explained it all earlier when she'd given him a lesson. He had listened, but now he couldn't remember the details.

Babies should come with a manual. A legal contract would be even better.

Gage walked with Hudson through the kitchen and back into the living room, copying what he'd seen Emma do. But, instead of resting his head on Gage's shoulder, Hudson arched back to study his new mode of transportation. The soft material of the navy blue footed pajamas Emma had changed him into stretched with the movement.

Hudson peered up with curious blue eyes. His hair held a hint of auburn, but mostly brown. His chubby fist grasped Gage's shirt near his collar. He didn't look tired. When Emma had been holding him, he had, but now?

Not even close.

"What are we going to do with each other?"

No answer. No smiles like Ruby had conjured.

Might as well lay him down and see what happened. Earlier today the crew at his house had set up a portable crib/playpen in his guest bedroom. Gage didn't have a permanent crib yet, and he wouldn't be needing one if things went according to plan.

He headed down the hall and into the bedroom, settling Hudson into the portable crib with his blanket and a stuffed elephant. Hudson stared as he backed away.

What now? Would he put himself to sleep?

Gage retreated to the master bedroom, giving his king-size bed a longing glance as he entered his bathroom. Could he risk sleeping in here tonight? What if Hudson cried and he couldn't hear him? Maybe he should have put the portable crib in his room for the first night. Was it too late for that?

A wail sounded as he rinsed his toothbrush and deposited it back into the holder.

Guess that answered his worry about being too far away. Even someone hard of hearing wouldn't be able to miss the tornado siren coming from across the hall.

He found Hudson twisted up with his blanket, as if he'd been rolling around and got stuck. Fat, sad tears rolled down the baby's cheeks, which had turned splotchy.

Gage pulled him out of the mess, snagged the blanket and held it against Hudson's back. What now? He walked into the living room. Hudson peered this way and that, probably looking for Emma. Or his dad. Or his nanny.

"I'm sorry you're stuck with me, buddy. I'd be upset, too. Are you hungry? Or not tired? What's going on?"

When did kids start talking? Hopefully, around nine months old, because Gage could use some answers from the tyke.

It might be worth trying to feed him. What could it hurt?

Gage somehow managed to make a bottle while holding Hudson, though numerous powder spills and drops of water lined the counter after the impressive feat.

He headed for the espresso leather recliner in the living room and sat. Hudson drank a little, then stared at him. Nibbled on the bottle a bit more. Emma had only fed him the hour before so he probably wasn't hungry, but Gage wasn't sure what else to do. He didn't have a lot of baby-whispering options up the sleeve of his waffle shirt.

He gave up on the bottle, setting it on the floor next to the chair.

Hudson's head rested in the crook of Gage's arm. His eyes flooded. A whimper escaped, followed by a cry.

All day, Gage had held himself in check. Not allowing himself to reflect on what Hudson had been through. What he'd lost. First his mother. Now his dad. It was too much for a baby to contend with. That's why Gage wanted to find him the perfect forever home, and fast. Hudson needed a mom and a dad. Ones who knew what they were doing. Who could give him the love he deserved and the family he needed.

"Your dad was my closest friend in law school." Like a rusty engine, Hudson's cry stuttered. "He was the kind of guy who would do anything for you."

Somehow, he'd gained the baby's rapt attention. And he wasn't about to lose it and have him start crying again, so Gage kept talking. "When things went bad with Nicole, he was there for me. I'm not sure I was as there for him when your mom—" Gage swallowed. "When she went to heaven. I tried, but I just…didn't know what I was doing."

If only Zeke hadn't attempted to outfly that storm, he'd be holding his son right now instead of an inept Gage.

Zeke had been rushing to get back from a meeting in Aspen. He'd had his pilot's license for years and was meticulous about following protocol. That's why the accident had come as such a shock. But he'd hurried through his preflight check in order to beat the weather and then encountered mechanical issues that could have been avoided.

Moisture coated Gage's eyes, and he blinked to clear

it away. If Hudson went to another home, would they keep Zeke's memory alive for the boy?

He'd never thought about that before.

Hudson's face contorted, and he howled again, adding some kicks of frustration. Gage understood the sentiment.

"There was this one time in school…"

Once again, Hudson paused to listen. Perhaps he was searching, hoping to hear his dad's voice. Either way, Gage kept talking. He told Hudson about his dad. He started with their first year of law school, and by the time he was three stories in, the boy was asleep.

Long lashes rested against his plump cheeks, body limp in Gage's arms. Sweet boy. Zeke and Leila had sure made a cute kid.

Gently, Gage eased the recliner footrest up. He didn't want to move and wake Hudson, so he'd close his eyes and rest here for a minute.

And maybe when he woke up, his life would make sense again.

Chapter Three

 $\mathbf{W}$ hy was her nose so cold? Had it frozen off her face?

Emma's hand snaked up, rubbing the extremity. Like a sleeping limb, it buzzed, attempting to return from the land of glaciers. Had the heat kicked off in the cabin during the night?

She scrounged for her blankets, recognition of her whereabouts quickly registering when she latched onto her car's steering wheel instead. A painful new kink in her neck made its presence known when she moved her seat to an upright position.

Emma scrambled for her phone. No messages or calls, so Gage and Hudson must be okay. And it was five in the morning.

Oops. The car was freezing, and so was she. She rubbed her arms through the sleeves of her down jacket. How could she have slept so long in such poor conditions?

"Birdie, I need you to start up nice and quiet now." Emma tapped the dash of her Mini Cooper. When she'd purchased it, an I See Birds sticker had adorned the bumper. She'd since removed it, but the birding phrase had prompted her to choose the name.

The car's engine, usually a gentle purr, roared. "Shh. Did you turn into a lion overnight? That's enough noise out of you." She kept her headlights off as she slowly eased down Gage's drive. Emma had no desire to wake anyone up or notify Gage that she'd slept in front of his house for the last few hours.

When she got back to the cabin, Emma snuck inside quietly, attempting not to disturb her sister, Mackenzie, who slept in the other bedroom.

She climbed into bed, the warmth a comfort, but couldn't shake the chill from her body. After about an hour of hoping sleep would come, she gave up and readied for the day. A hot shower and a cup of tea did wonders for bringing her back to normal temps. She dressed in a black T-shirt—Best Aunt Ever scrawled across it in white print—along with skinny jeans and a long, comfortable cardigan.

She was sitting at the small kitchen table, nursing a second cup of tea, eating toast and reading her morning devotions when Mackenzie came out of her room in pajama bottoms and an old T-shirt sporting their high school mascot—a mustang. Even groggy and half-awake, Mackenzie was long and willowy and strong and feminine all at the same time.

Emma had gotten used to their sister roles long ago. She was of the plain and simple variety and liked reading, tea and binging on chick flicks. Mackenzie was far more adventurous, always needing to conquer the next thing. She could be found white-water rafting or taking bull riding lessons. Actually, she hadn't tried that last thing. Yet.

"Hey, you're up early." Mackenzie shuffled to the coffeepot and gazed longingly at it as if sheer desire might make the necessary contents jump inside.

"Didn't sleep great this morning. I'm about to head back over to Gage's. See if he and Hudson survived the night."

"That's right." Mackenzie removed the coffee from the freezer and filled the reusable filter with grounds, then added water from the pitcher in the fridge. The girl liked her coffee a certain way, so Emma never attempted to make it for her. "I'm sure they were fine. Gage will do great with him," she added with a dismissive wave.

Her sister didn't have the same concern over Gage and the baby that Emma did. But then, she hadn't been the one to encourage Gage to keep Hudson in the first place when he'd wanted to find someone else right away.

He'd tried, though. Right now there weren't any other options. So Emma really hadn't pushed him into a decision he wouldn't have come to on his own.

"Still, I should get over there. You know how hard taking care of a baby can be."

Mackenzie got out a mug with the new Wilder Ranch logo that Cate had recently designed. None of the mugs in their cupboard matched, and Emma liked it that way. Each morning she picked out one that best fit her day. Her mood. Today hers was one she'd made in ceramics class back in high school. Just the right size but a little off-kilter.

Her sister covered a yawn. "Not really."

True. Mackenzie didn't involve herself much with the Kids' Club that Emma ran. And when they'd been younger, Emma had babysat a ton while Mackenzie had given riding lessons to earn spending money.

The two of them were night-and-day different but managed to get along. For that, Emma was thankful.

She cleared her dishes and said goodbye to her sister, then hopped back into her car, which still held a bit of the warmth from when she'd driven it home early this morning.

When she arrived at Gage's, the time on her dash read seven thirty. It was crazy early in the morning to arrive at someone's house, but she doubted Gage would complain.

Emma grabbed her purse and her to-go mug of steeping tea. Three cups was more than her norm, but she needed the extra—albeit small—boost of caffeine it would offer.

She stood on the step of Gage's sprawling ranch house and knocked lightly. It had been his uncle's ranch until a few years ago. Kip Frasier. A quiet but sweet man who always kept candy in his pocket at church and would dole it out to kids. He'd never married or had children of his own. When he'd passed away, he'd left the ranch to Gage. People really liked to leave things to the man. Land. House. Baby.

Gage had lived here only a little over two years.

The door swung open. Gage's hair was damp as if he'd recently showered, and he wore a plaid shirt unbuttoned over a white T-shirt with jeans and leather slippers.

Gage Frasier, you are one attractive man.

One who, unfortunately, didn't see her as anything more than a neighbor or his friend's little sister. Emma wasn't even on his datable radar.

The only good part about Gage not being interested in her in *that* way—besides the fact that she'd never be able to give up on the dream of having children—was that she wouldn't have to admit to him that she had something in common with his ex-wife.

Before Nicole had run off with James the Homewrecker, Emma had dated him.

The whole ordeal was embarrassing. Mortifying. She'd been so naive and foolish. Emma should have known immediately that everything James spouted was a lie—as if anyone would ever find her as irresistible as he had claimed she was—but she'd allowed herself to be swept away by his flattering words and gestures. He'd been as fake and slimy as the toy goo her niece Ruby liked to play with.

"Morning." Gage's voice had that scratchy, unused-as-of-yet quality.

"How's Hudson? How'd the night go? Did either of you sleep?"

His mouth tugged up at the corners, and her girlish hopes and dreams gave a collective sigh at what would never be. "Come in, Emma."

She did, the quiet click of the door sounding behind her. There was no sign of the baby anywhere...

She took off her coat, and Gage hung it in the front closet, storing her purse, too. She set her tea on the entry table as Gage motioned for her to follow him. They walked down the hall and into the guest bedroom. With beige walls and a simple olive green bedspread on the full-size bed, the room was masculine. If Hudson stayed, she'd offer to help redo it into something more fitting for a baby boy. Maybe with a vintage airplane theme in honor of his father, Zeke. A nice framed sketch or two, with a light blue color on the walls. Brown accents.

Getting ahead of yourself, girl. Rein it in.

Emma didn't even know how the night had gone, and here she was, planning the future.

Hudson was asleep on his back in the portable crib, one chubby hand above his head in a fist like he was cheering in victory. As if sensing their presence, his eyelids fluttered, then opened.

"What a good boy you are! You slept in your own bed? Such a big boy." Emma had him in her arms before he could consider crying.

"Actually, he slept with me in the recliner for most of the night." Visions of Hudson snoozing on Gage's chest made her own constrict.

Was there a more attractive picture than that?

Emma laid him on the bed and proceeded to change his diaper while he studied both her and Gage. Hudson arched his back when she tried to put his footie pajamas back on his feet, so she tickled his tummy, distracting him so that she could finish the task.

"Are you hungry?" Emma asked Hudson as she picked him back up.

"Ba."

"Ba," she repeated back to him. "That could mean yes. Or no. Or nothing." Her amusement earned a drowsy smile from him in return. "Do you like scrambled eggs?" Those were soft. Or he might prefer a bottle or pureed baby food. "Let's go figure out some breakfast."

The three of them moved into the kitchen. "Here." She handed the baby to Gage and retrieved the eggs from the fridge. She knew they'd be inside because she'd asked Mackenzie to pick up groceries yesterday morning to leave at Gage's. Just in case he didn't have much. He was, after all, a guy. And based on past conversations, she didn't think Gage was much of a cook.

Gage held Hudson facing out so he could see his surroundings. Still not perfectly at ease, but better than last night. "Andrea—his previous nanny—already texted this morning to check on him."

"That was nice of her."

"Definitely. I told her he's doing well. Not that I knew exactly how he would wake up. But at least then you'd be here, so I wouldn't have to worry."

"Sounds like you two did great." Emma flashed a grin at Hudson as she made her way to the stove with the eggs and a carton of milk. He kicked and waved his arms in answer. "Sweet boy." She leaned in, pressing numerous kisses to his forehead. "If you slept all night, I bet you're hungry."

Emma turned to Gage's cupboards and scrounged for a bowl, hiding a megawatt smile. It had worked! Her plan to abandon Gage and Hudson had panned out.

Gage hadn't answered all of the questions she'd lobbed at him while on his front step, but he wasn't a haggard mess. He'd managed a shower. That had to be a good sign.

Emma had hoped and prayed Hudson would sleep well. She'd also anticipated some fussiness or possibly a meltdown—from him or Gage. But the scenario she'd walked into this morning was way better than she'd imagined.

Maybe convincing Gage to keep the baby would be easier than she'd thought.

"He didn't exactly sleep all night."

Emma cracked an egg and emptied it into the glass bowl, placing the shell on a paper towel. "Oh, he didn't? That's a bummer. So what happened? Did he cry?"

"He woke up at about five."

Her hand froze midcrack on the second egg, clear liquid sliding down the outside of the glass bowl. She finished dumping in what was left, then wiped up the spill with a paper towel. After foraging a piece of shell out of the eggs, she tossed the paper towel and shell into the trash.

"I heard a noise around then."

Emma's head whipped in his direction, panic dancing in her silver-blue eyes. "You did? What was it? Ouch." Her fingers dug into the side of her neck as she faced the counter again.

"A vehicle, and I don't think it would have been one of the guys. Too early. Do you have a knot?"

"Yeah, but it's not a big deal. So…you didn't see who it was?"

"No. When I moved, Hudson roused. I fed him a bottle and he went back to sleep. That's when I laid him in his bed."

"Oh, what a relief."

That was a strange response. Unless… It couldn't have been Emma he'd heard this morning, could it? But why would she be here at that hour?

Gage switched Hudson to his left arm. "Let me." He took over massaging the knot for her. The faint hint of something sweet—like vanilla or cinnamon—teased his senses. His stomach rumbled, thankfully quietly, in response. To the idea of food or Emma herself?

The first, of course. Emma was too young for him and too…pristine. Like a dish someone would put on a high shelf and then never use. He was world-weary and disheartened regarding relationships—like an old, dirty slop bucket used for feeding pigs. The two items didn't belong in the same vicinity. Emma deserved a fresh relationship with a man who hadn't been through what he had. Who wasn't jaded. And who wanted kids.

Strange that his mind had even traveled in that direction regarding her. He'd known her for a couple of years and it never had before.

"You don't need to do that." Emma motioned to his kneading, while at the same time relaxing her neck in the other direction to allow him access. "But it feels really good." Since Emma faced the counter, she couldn't see his amused grin. He liked how the truth rolled from her tongue, often, it seemed, without her permission.

Except at this moment, when she was acting a bit elusive.

"Thanks for the massage." Emma returned to the eggs, cracking and adding two more. "Well, I'm glad it wasn't worse, that Hudson wasn't up every hour or two."

Dread rolled through him. "Babies do that?"

"They can when they're little. Probably not at this age, but with all he's been through...not impossible. Especially with the new surroundings."

"So how'd you sleep last night?"

"Great." The word reeked of fake perkiness. "Where's your frying pan?"

He pointed with the toe of his leather slipper to the lower cupboard. She found a small one, then sprayed it with oil and set it on the burner.

Hudson squirmed in his arms, and Gage put him on the floor. He crawled across the kitchen to the dining table and began inspecting a chair. He put a hand on the bottom rung and attempted to pull up, then wobbled and dropped back to the ground. Confusion and worry puckered his little brow as he made his way back to them. Poor kid. Everything was new and different for him.

I miss your dad, too, little guy. I wish I was more like him. But, I promise, I am going to find the right family for you.

Emma beat the eggs, then sent them careening into the pan. It *whooshed* as the mixture hit the heated surface.

When Hudson gave a disgruntled cry, Emma turned to him. "Oh, kiddo, you're so out of your element. We need to unpack the rest of your toys this morning." She opened a lower cupboard and retrieved a large metal mixing bowl, then a plastic serving spoon from the utensil drawer. Once she handed them to Hudson, he contentedly made a racket with the two items.

Gage leaned against the counter, facing Emma as she stirred the eggs in the pan. She didn't look at him.

"Anything I can do to help?"

"Nope. This is too easy to require assistance." After finishing the eggs, she turned off the burner, carrying the pan over to Hudson's high chair. She used the spatula to spread some of the scrambled eggs onto the tray and then blew across them. Once she returned the pan to the stove, she scooped Hudson up from the floor and transported him to the high chair.

"Do you want some eggs? Does that sound good?" She buckled him in, securing a bib around his neck. He fisted a handful of food and maneuvered it, not so gracefully, into his mouth.

Emma got a plate out of the cupboard next to Gage. "Hungry?" She nodded toward the pan. "I made enough for you."

"And you?"

"No. I already ate."

She moved to the utensil drawer, but Gage beat her to the spot, blocking her from opening it. "Emma, what were you doing around five this morning?"

"Sleeping." Her answer came out fast, but it slipped up at the end, almost a question.

"So there's no way it was your car I heard, right?"

Her profile stayed stoic for all of three seconds before cracking into something near embarrassment. "Before I left last night, I wanted to wait it out. Make sure there wasn't an emergency or that you didn't need me right away. And then I fell asleep in my car."

"Are you serious?" His voice dialed up to a nine. She'd slept out there almost all night? In the cold?

"I promise it wasn't planned. And I'm so sorry I woke you. If I hadn't, Hudson might have kept sleeping." She huffed. "It was stupid of me to let that happen."

"It was stupid, but not because you woke me. I could care less about that. And I'm not worried about Hudson being up for a few minutes. He did great. But I am concerned about you. Emma, you can't be doing stuff like that. You need to take care of yourself. Hudson and I will be fine. And I'll call you if we're not. Okay?"

Her mouth pursed to one side. "I just…needed to make sure the two of you were good. And it truly was an accident. Okay?" A grin tempered the cheeky mimicked addition, seasoning it sweet.

The brittle parts of him softened. It was hard to stay upset around Emma. She just sort of…diffused him.

"Next time you pull something like that, I'm going to put you in a time-out."

Her laughter brightened the room as much as a strand of twinkling white Christmas lights.

What was he going to do with this woman? How could

Emma be so considerate and selfless? It was starkly different from anything Gage had ever experienced with Nicole. After they'd married, his ex-wife had pretty much focused on herself. He had hoped that the tendency would change with age and maturity, but it hadn't.

Nicole had put her needs above everyone else's. She would never have watched out for Hudson—and him— the way Emma did.

When Gage had told Emma yesterday that he planned to pay her for watching the baby, she'd thrown a royal fit. He still would…somehow. But in her mind, she was just volunteering at this point. Before Hudson had come into his life, Gage had known that Emma and Nicole were nothing alike. That they couldn't even be classified in the same category.

But the last few days had only highlighted their differences.

One was sunshine. Just her presence made breathing easier. The other was pneumonia—stealing his oxygen. Wreaking havoc like a storm that wouldn't quit raging.

Turns out he was quite partial to bright blue skies and cloudless days.

Chapter Four

The front door of the house opened, and Emma glanced up as Gage let himself in, stomping a light dusting of snow from his boots and brushing it from his hair.

"Look who's here!" Emma spoke to Hudson, who was sitting on the floor in front of the coffee table with her, a smattering of blocks, baby toys and a ball between them.

Hudson tilted forward, banging his hands against the cowhide rug. "La-la-la-ba-ba." He blew bubbles as Gage took off his boots, finished hanging up his coat and joined them.

"Ba to you, too." Gage created a human triangle and rolled the red plastic ball to Hudson. The boy tried shoving it in his mouth. Thankfully, the medium size allowed him to grip it easily but not insert it.

It had been six days since Hudson's arrival, and Emma had spent copious amounts of time playing with him and holding him during the week. Anything to make the transition smoother.

"How come when you roll the ball to him, he doesn't eat it?"

"He does a lot of the time." Emma lifted the white

burp cloth from the floor next to her. "I've been wiping off slobber when he wants to play again."

Gage's nose wrinkled. "Am I allowed to say yuck?"

"You're only allotted two complaints of disgust in a day, so I'd suggest saving it for diaper-changing time."

His cheeks curved. "True."

The ball shot out of Hudson's grip, and Emma returned it to him before he could complain. Back into his mouth it went. The boy had to be teething the way he chewed on everything around him. "How was your day? How are ranch-y things?"

Gage's chuckle messed with her midsection. Like she'd overloaded on something delicious and her body couldn't decide how to respond.

"You do realize you grew up on a ranch, right?"

"A guest ranch is different. We don't even have cattle year-round, as you well know." They only had them for the guests to move in the summer, and nothing like the size of Gage's operation.

"Another one of the ranchers from church dropped by today to tell me—in the spirit of helpfulness, of course—that I'm crazy for changing things around here the way I have. They think I'm messing up everything my uncle did because I switched to summer calving. But it's helped me cut down on everything—cowboys, supplemental feed. Plus, the profit will be better because they're fattening up faster."

"It's really amazing to me that you've done so well with ranching."

He waved off her compliment. "Ford is a great teacher. And he didn't even balk after I researched summer calving and decided I wanted to try it. We could have always gone back to the way things were if it didn't pan out. But so far it's been great. And…there I go again, boring you with ranching details."

"Actually, I like listening to you talk about it." Emma wanted to hear just about anything Gage had to say, and it had nothing to do with the smooth timbre of his voice or the way his brow wrinkled in concentration when he spoke about something he was passionate about. Those were just lovely little side benefits.

"That's because you're way too nice."

Hudson dropped the ball, then crawled over to Emma's lap. She picked him up, nibbling on his cheeks. "There's some leftover macaroni and cheese. I made homemade for lunch. You're welcome to it."

Those lake-blue eyes of his narrowed to slits. "Please tell me you didn't bring over the ingredients to cook again."

"I didn't. I may have grocery shopped for here, but I put everything for your house on your tab at Len's, just like you made me promise to do." The contract he'd written up was on the fridge. And, yes, he'd made her sign it.

Gage had turned all serious, so Emma raised her right hand like she was taking an oath. "Promise."

"Good girl."

She stifled a groan. That was exactly how he thought of her, wasn't it?

Emma put Hudson down, and he crawled into Gage's lap. Gage picked him up, holding him against his chest. Their slightly awkward interactions were endearing. Each day Gage's actions were smoother, less rehearsed. And Hudson was following his lead. Their relationship had been warming at Crock-Pot speeds.

Emma still wouldn't mind that camera to see what happened around here in the evening, though. Gage didn't complain, but it sounded like Hudson often woke at least once a night. What she wouldn't give to be a fly on the wall.

"So what are you two up to tonight?"

Gage placed Hudson back on the floor, then built a stack of blocks for him to knock down. "Pretty much this. It hasn't even been a full week since Hudson arrived. I haven't gotten used to adding anything else in yet."

"So you don't go anywhere at night after I leave?"

"Nope." Gage rebuilt the tower when Hudson squawked. "How can I? I'm barely handling this." He motioned between himself and Hudson.

"But you guys are doing so well together."

"We're doing okay, but I don't want to rock the boat."

Emma understood his reasoning; at the same time, if Gage never left the house with Hudson, never found any sense of normalcy in going out and doing regular, everyday things, then how would he ever come to the conclusion that he should keep the baby?

And Emma was already witnessing a difference in Gage. It might be slight, but the softening and refining had begun, thanks to Hudson.

If he got out more, maybe he'd see that he could have a life and keep Hudson, too.

"The two of you should come with me to the talent show at church tonight."

Ruby was participating in the Wednesday night church club talent show, and she'd been practicing her selection for weeks. Emma had already heard her poem more times than she could count because every time Ruby said, "Aunt Emma, do you want to listen to my poem?" Emma answered in the affirmative. At this point she had the whole thing memorized, but she wouldn't miss the final product for anything.

Gage's mouth tugged to one side. "Of course I'd like to see Ruby do her thing, but I don't want to mess up our rhythm." He nodded toward Hudson, who had crawled under the coffee table and was trying to back himself out of the predicament. So far he wasn't complaining, so Emma left him to figure it out on his own if he could.

"Hudson would enjoy it, too. The kids have been working hard. He'll be totally entertained." Maybe *totally* was a stretch.

"You think?"

"He loves Ruby."

"That's true. But who doesn't?"

Emma laughed. "She is precious. You should come tonight. Try it. You can always head home if it doesn't work."

"I'll think about it."

"Are you just saying that so that I'll stop bugging you about it?"

"Maybe."

She chuckled. "Fine. I'm done."

Emma said goodbye to Hudson—who had extracted himself from the table, smart boy—with a smattering of kisses and a tight hug. She gathered her things and put on her coat and shoes, then paused with a hand on the front doorknob. "I'll see you later tonight. It starts at six thirty." She scooted outside and shut the door before Gage could reiterate that he wasn't planning to come.

Getting him out of the house to prove that he could manage an extracurricular activity with Hudson in tow was worth a shot.

And of course it had everything to do with that and nothing to do with seeing him again.

Gage scooped another mound of pureed peas onto the baby spoon, then deposited the load into Hudson's mouth. The boy shuddered, then swallowed.

"I don't blame you for not liking them. They don't smell—or look—very good." On the next bite, Gage added a taste of applesauce like he'd seen Emma do. That was better received.

The Bluetooth speaker on the kitchen counter shuffle-played Drew Holcomb and The Neighbors songs, but the house was too quiet.

Like it always was after Emma took off in the evening.

"What should we do tonight? Another round of knocking down towers? Or maybe we'll read some books." One full box of Hudson's things had been children's books. Zeke must have read to him often, because the baby was surprisingly content to sit in Gage's lap and listen. He studied the pictures and touched the pages and babbled in his own little language. Reading before bedtime had become their norm.

Crazy to think it had only been six days since he'd moved Hudson to the ranch. Life had become a whirlwind of diapers and stinted sleep. Gage's mind had been in constant prayer mode. *Please comfort Hudson. Don't let me mess up his life in the time he's here. Help me find the right home for him. And thank You for Emma.*

No way would he or Hudson be surviving any of this without her. When she arrived in the mornings, Gage's muscles relaxed like overcooked pasta noodles. Hudson greeted her with waving arms and megagrins.

Emma made everything better. She couldn't help it. It was just the effect she had on the world.

That had to be why his house felt so empty when she left.

Gage finished feeding Hudson, wiped his face and hands, removed his bib and plucked him from the high chair. It was six o'clock. He'd been putting Hudson to bed around eight—at Emma's suggestion—and the schedule had been working.

"Well?" Gage held Hudson, tapping a finger against his nose, which Hudson promptly caught and then attempted to eat. "What's our plan? Do you want to get out of the house? Go to the talent show and see Ruby?" Hudson's two bottom teeth pressed into the flesh of Gage's finger, and he removed it from the baby's grasp, wiping the slobber on his jeans.

Maybe Emma was right. Gage could use a night out. And Hudson lit up around Ruby. Surely a bunch of performing kids would hold his attention for a little bit.

Plus, Emma would be there, so Gage would have help with the baby. And her company. "One later night won't hurt, will it?" He'd make sure they were home by eight thirty or nine at the latest.

Hudson crawled around Gage's room while he laced up his leather boots and changed into a button-down checked shirt. The boy was dressed in a onesie that proclaimed he was "cute as a button"—true story—along with soft pants made of the same material. He wore socks that resembled tennis shoes, and since he couldn't walk yet, Gage assumed shoes weren't necessary.

The drive to the church was uneventful, and Gage's lungs leaked with relief when they arrived unscathed.

They'd managed step one. Now on to the next. Should he take the car seat in? Or unbuckle Hudson?

Questions like this shouldn't be so hard, but he was a newbie. Gage decided to rescue Hudson from the car seat since the boy didn't love being strapped into it. He tugged a winter hat on him and wrapped him in his blanket in lieu of a coat. The idea of wrestling the little monkey into a jacket didn't appeal to him.

He and Hudson arrived in the sanctuary just as the children's director was making announcements. They should probably sit in the back so he could escape at the first sign of trouble.

But then Emma waved at him from near the front. The skin around her eyes crinkled, her lips bowed and she looked like home. How could he resist? Gage hurried to their row, greeting Luc, Cate and Mackenzie as he scooted past all of them to the open seat next to Emma. Had she saved him a spot? Based on the packed pews, he'd say yes.

"I'd just about given up on you two." Hudson lunged into her arms, and she removed his hat and smoothed the static from his hair. "Hey there, handsome." She smooched Hudson's cheek, creating a noise that made him giggle.

Emma had changed her clothes since she'd been at Gage's. She wore black leggings and boots, a loose wrap with dotted shirtsleeves peeking out. Her hair was down, tempting him to explore the level of softness, and, to top it all off, the woman smelled like dessert. Sweet. Cinnamon.

Gage leaned in her direction as he took off his coat, skin tingling at the close proximity to her. "You changed clothes."

That's what came out of his mouth? He'd been aiming for more of a compliment than an observation.

"I had Hudson drool and a bit of plum on my shirt from today, so…" Her shoulders lifted.

"You look really nice." There. That was better. Though pretty would have been a more fitting—albeit trouble-inducing—description.

Her chin jutted back slightly in surprise. "Thanks." And then the lilting lips were back, mesmerizing him for a full three seconds. Emma had really great, full lips. She rarely wore anything on them, but tonight they were glossy and as distracting to him as earrings were to Hudson. The boy was currently going at Emma's like a cat after a laser light.

She slipped them free from her ears. "Can you hold these?" She dropped the silver dangles into his hand. His fist closed around them as the first performer took the stage and Emma's attention registered up front.

Gage tucked them into his front shirt pocket. How could something as simple as Emma removing her earrings without complaint intrigue him so much? She would do anything for Hudson—or really anyone—without a second thought. Emma loved big. She'd make a great mom one day. And an amazing wife. Surprising there wasn't a line of men at her door waiting to ask her out.

Come to think of it, Gage didn't hear much about her dating at all. Why not? Emma was a catch. For someone more fitting, of course. But he could observe, couldn't he? As long as he didn't get any crazy ideas that they were right for each other.

He could just imagine what Luc would have to say about that. No way would he consider Gage, with his messy past and cynical attitude about love, a match for sweet, innocent Emma.

The first couple of talents—a juggler, a tap dancer, a little girl who sang remarkably well and then one who sang precisely the opposite—all went by pretty quickly. Hudson got passed down the row, and Cate held him for a bit. When Ruby walked onstage, she sent the baby back their way so she could record the performance. Emma kept Hudson when he made it to her. She retrieved a teething ring from the diaper bag, and Hudson chewed on it.

Before Ruby started, she waved at Luc and Cate, then her aunts, as if greeting her fans before she could proceed. Cate laughed, whispering something in Luc's ear. Man, what a change. The two of them had turned a one-eighty, completely renewing their relationship in a way that Gage hadn't thought possible.

Almost made him believe second chances could actually happen. But Luc and Cate were the exception, not the rule. Plus, if anyone deserved to rebuild a future together, it was them.

Gage, on the other hand, carried too much blame for what had transpired between himself and Nicole. During their short marriage, Gage had prayed and hoped that they would gel. Mature.

Love each other with a selfless kind of love. But their relationship had quickly turned rocky. Nicole had begun spending time with friends he didn't know. Not telling him where she was going or when. And when he'd tried reaching out to her, she'd closed off.

She'd become self-focused. Demanding. Bitter.

Hard to love.

He'd tried to save them, but he hadn't been enough.

Gage still wasn't sure how it had all gone so off course so quickly. Only that he'd failed. They'd failed. And he wasn't sure he believed in his ability to make a marriage successful.

Ruby finished her poem and the audience applauded. Hudson lunged from Emma's arms to his. Gage held him facing forward, and Hudson stood on his thighs. His legs held for a few seconds at a time, then sagged. They repeated the dance a few times, and then Hudson cocked back and chucked his toy ring toward the pew in front of them. The tossing in and of itself wasn't that much of a surprise because everything was a hazard in Hudson's grip. But the fact that it beaned an elderly woman on the shoulder was downright mortifying. Hopefully, she'd be gracious since it was obviously an accident.

The woman's chin whipped over her shoulder, and her glare about cut him in two. Of course Hudson hadn't messed with just anyone. It was ol' Mrs. Carp. The woman had been terrifying children with her high standards and expectations since the eighteen hundreds, at least. She must be here to see her great-grandchildren perform.

Gage grimaced. "I'm so sorry."

After letting out a growl-hiss combination directed squarely at Gage and his obvious lack of control over a nine-month-old baby, Mrs. Carp whirled to face the front again.

Emma, who had conveniently disappeared during the exchange, rose up from her crouched-over position.

"Ah, thanks for leaving me hanging."

"What?" Emma's fingertips landed against her sternum, attempting surprise. "I had to get his teething ring from the floor." Her shoulders shook with suppressed laughter as she handed the ring to Hudson.

"Your whole doe-eyed expression isn't going to work on me, woman. I've got your number."

A laugh burst out of her. She slapped a hand over her mouth to stifle it, but it bubbled up, seeped through the cracks. Gage's chest rumbled in response. Mrs. Carp would not approve of such revelry. They even earned pinched brows and curious looks from Mackenzie and Cate. Their laughter quieted, but something in Gage had already broken free. When he'd been a teenager, he'd had a nasty flu that had taken him out, and he'd slept for sixteen hours at the tail end, finally waking up to some semblance of normalcy the next morning. Lungs functioning again. Head not being squeezed to oblivion inside a giant-sized vise.

Alive.

That's how Emma made him feel.

Hudson let out a cry. He'd dropped his toy onto the pew, but this time when Emma offered it back to him his arms flailed, head shaking. He kicked, face twisting, and then he screamed.

Not good.

Emma reached for him, and Hudson balked, bending away from her grip, his cry escalating. The program was almost over, but the poor boy onstage playing the piano was getting drowned out.

Gage had to get out of the sanctuary. He stood, snagged the diaper bag and his coat, then scooted down the row, Hudson flailing in his arms. The backpack bumped into everyone as he tripped out of the pew and then barely resisted a flat-out run for the back of the church.

Hudson only paused his crying once on the way out, and unfortunately, it was to reload his lungs and then do the impossible—up the volume. Gage crashed out of the sanctuary and into the meeting hall connected to it. Not far enough.

He exited the church, Hudson's livid howl filling the otherwise silent night. In his hurry, he'd forgotten Hudson's blanket, but there was no way he was going back for it now. Gage bundled him inside his jacket and jogged to his SUV.

What was wrong with the boy? He'd been fed plenty before they'd left for church. And he'd been changed. Gage lifted him and sniffed his diapered bottom like he'd seen mothers do on occasion. He'd always thought the move strange, but now considered it pure survival. No stinky odors wafted toward him, but Hudson's cry remained despondent.

Maybe the car ride home would quiet him. Gage dropped the diaper bag on the ground and opened Hudson's door.

"Gage." Emma called, hurrying across the parking lot toward him. "Hey, are you okay?" She had Hudson's blanket in her hands.

Hudson's cry grated like bare skin kissing cement at top speeds. "Nope." This was exactly why he hadn't wanted to leave the house tonight. He should have followed his instincts.

"Do you want me to try with him?"

"It's okay. We're just going to head home."

He tossed his coat on the floor and placed Hudson in the car seat, and the tantrum upped ten notches. Hudson arched so that Gage couldn't close the buckle. Finally he got the squirmy bundle locked in, but Gage's efforts were on par with the energy required for wrangling calves.

"Do you think he's hungry? Or has a dirty diaper?"

Emma peered into the car seat, a hand on Hudson's sock-covered foot. "It's okay, baby. You're all right." Her cooing tone didn't make a dent in Hurricane Hudson.

"I fed and changed him right before we came. And I just took a whiff of his diaper. It was fine." Gage shut the back door. "Hopefully, if I drive he'll calm down."

"I'm so sorry."

He hopped into the front seat as Hudson's cry took on a panicked note. "You don't have to feel guilty for encouraging us to come, Emma." *Even though my gut was right.* "We'll be fine." He hoped.

Gage tore out of the lot. The spurt of speed earned him momentary silence from Hudson, and then the crying kicked back in with renewed strength.

Gage could only hope and pray he wasn't in for a long night. Because Hudson hadn't been this upset since he'd arrived at the ranch. And Gage—despite all of Emma's encouragement—still didn't know what he was doing.

Chapter Five

Gage walked with Hudson.

He bounced. Tried the activity saucer. Sippy cup with juice. Numerous toys. A book. A movie. He changed the baby's diaper. Attempted to feed him a bottle, which he gargled and refused to drink.

Nothing worked.

The boy was bent on screaming, and there wasn't anything Gage could do about it. It was as if everything had come to a head—the loss of his dad, his nanny, any sign of his normal life. Hudson was having a meltdown, and Gage didn't blame the poor kid.

He'd read something about laying a baby down and letting them cry it out, but he didn't think that was the answer. Hudson was too mad. And Gage couldn't handle listening to the shrill sound without at least attempting to comfort him.

At this point, he was starting to think Hudson might wail until he turned two.

Gage's phone signaled a text from the vicinity of the kitchen. He walked in that direction to check it, but Hudson's pause in crying made him screech to a halt. The baby had caught sight of his own reflection in the back sliding glass doors. Gage moved closer so he could check it out, but when they neared, Hudson's face wrinkled and the complaints kicked back into high gear.

Disappointment squeezed Gage's lungs.

For the next half hour, he continued to do everything he could think of, and Hudson continued to howl.

Gage hated to abandon the boy, even for a second, but he had to use the restroom. He walked into the guest room and laid Hudson in the portable crib.

The screaming escalated, Hudson's legs and arms kicking and flailing. "I'll be right back, buddy. Promise."

He hurried into the hall bathroom while Hudson roared. When he returned, the boy's face was bright red and sopping wet from all of the tears. "If you keep this up, little guy, I just might join you. I'm not sure I'll ever understand what your dad was thinking picking me for this." But then, Zeke had likely never imagined that the stopgaps he'd set in place in case of an emergency would actually be used.

Gage scooped up Hudson and returned to the living room. "I'm not sure what else to do for you, but I can hold you. That's about all I've got left for ideas." He wiped Hudson's face with a burp cloth, and the baby hiccuped, his breath coming in spurts as he tried to catch it. Gage settled onto the couch, feeling as if he'd run a marathon tonight. He held Hudson and patted his back, praying silently as he let the boy get it all out.

Eventually—in what may have been minutes but felt like hours—his screams quieted and his hiccups subsided. Heavy eyelids drooped and opened, then shuttered again.

The two of them stayed right where they were, Gage

more certain than ever that he was the wrong choice to be Hudson's guardian. How could he raise a baby on his own?

He couldn't even manage one night out.

"Let me see your phone." Cate held her hand out toward Emma from the other end of the couch. The two of them had been hanging out at Cate and Luc's house since the program. Ruby and Luc had gone to bed, but Cate was a good enough friend to stay up and overanalyze with Emma. "How many texts have you sent Gage since he left church? Are we leaning toward obsessive at this point?"

Emma groaned and most certainly did not hand over her phone. "Five."

"Five?" Cate's volume shot to deafening levels. "What all did you say?"

"Hey." Luc's voice came through the main floor bedroom door. "Keep it down out there. Some of us are trying to sleep."

"And some of us are trying to have a conversation! Not everyone goes to bed this early, old man!" Emma's little-sister retort was answered by a groan from Luc and the sound of a soft object—probably a pillow—hitting the bedroom door.

She and Cate laughed, Emma's ending with a snort that increased their giggles.

Despite teasing Luc, Emma kept her volume low to answer Cate's earlier question. "First I asked Gage if he was okay, then I asked if he needed help, and then I offered to drive over there." Their cat, Princess Prim, jumped up on the couch and curled into Emma's side. She stroked its fur, earning a purr of contentment. When

Luc and Prim had first become acquainted, the cat had tortured him. And she'd seemed to enjoy every second. But now that Prim had accepted Luc was a permanent fixture in her life, she'd allowed him to become one of her doting human servants.

"That's three." Cate's eyebrows reached for her dark chocolate hairline. "What were the other two texts?"

"One was an apology for making him go out tonight and the other said I was praying for them."

Cate's exhale was coupled with a shaking head, cheeks creasing. "You didn't make him go to the talent show, and you didn't do anything wrong, Emma. You were trying to help."

But had she been? Or had her motives been on the selfish side? Her getting to see Gage and Hudson. Gage keeping Hudson. "Do you think I should just go over there?"

"No." Not a hint of doubt laced Cate's answer. "I'm sure everything is fine by now."

"Then why hasn't he answered me?" Emma had been glued to her phone since Gage had torn out of the church parking lot.

Cate sipped her tea, absentmindedly rubbing her growing tummy. "They'll be fine. What's the worst that can happen?"

Emma's eyes supersized. "So many things. Probably not the question to be asking me right now."

"Eventually, Hudson will stop crying. He'll fall asleep or become too exhausted to continue the fit. But I doubt that's even happening. He probably calmed down on the way home. I'm sure Gage is just getting him to bed or has fallen asleep himself. Which is why—" Cate motioned to the phone "—he hasn't answered your texts yet. You offered to drive over and help. He hasn't responded. He'll accept if he needs you. I think you have to let it go."

Emma's teeth pressed into her lip. "I'm not very good at that."

Cate laughed. "Welcome to the club." She followed the comment with a yawn. One that reminded Emma that she should let Cate get to bed. The poor woman had been so worn-out lately.

"I think we'd both better get some sleep." Emma loaded their mugs into the dishwasher, then gave her sister-in-law a hug before hoofing it up the hill to her cabin.

The sound of gunfire greeted her as she stepped inside. Mackenzie had on another one of her old Western movies. For each romantic movie Emma consumed, Mackenzie watched something with cowboys and gunfights. And—Emma peered around to the front of the couch—she often managed to fall asleep despite the noise levels. Tonight was no different. Emma rounded the sofa, moving the blanket from the back of the couch so that it covered Kenzie.

In an attempt to keep herself from walking back out of the cabin and driving over to check on Hudson and Gage, Emma changed into pajamas. She removed her makeup and tossed her hair up into a messy bun. But even her gray jammies covered in charcoal zebras wouldn't keep her from zooming straight over to Gage's if he asked her for help.

If only the man would text to say they were okay. Or send a smoke signal. Something. Anything to ease her current agitation.

After brushing her teeth, Emma returned to her room and checked her phone. Still no message. The night flashed by in spurts of sleep and worry. Dreams that included Gage ending up at the emergency room with a crying Hudson. A new family coming to take Hudson and Emma not getting the chance to say goodbye.

Three was the last number she recalled seeing on her alarm clock, and then bright sun streamed in through her blinds. While she was thankful she'd finally slept, panic set in. Now was the time she usually arrived at Gage's.

Emma tore out of bed.

She dressed in a burgundy wraparound sweatshirt with leggings and lined ankle rain boots. After brushing her teeth and winding her hair up into a bun, she skipped breakfast or tea, instead heading over to Gage's.

At Emma's knock, Gage called for her to come in. She opened the door, taking her first real breath when she saw Hudson in the high chair, Gage feeding him. She dropped her purse to the floor and pitched her coat on top, then crossed over to them. Her hand rested on Gage's shoulder as she bent to kiss and smell Hudson's sweet head. Baby shampoo with the faint hint of last night's dinner. Nothing better.

"You're both okay." With the flip of a switch, Emma's respiratory system began functioning again. She didn't remove her hand from Gage's shoulder. His long-sleeved flannel shirt was warm and comforting under her fingertips because he was in it. And just like she needed to see Hudson was all right, she needed to know the same about Gage.

"Barely." Amusement danced across Gage's features, and Emma swallowed a sigh of girlish attraction. If he'd had a tough night, the man didn't show it. He was as handsome as ever. Emma had been so rushed this morning that she hadn't put on makeup. Probably looked as if she'd just rolled out of bed. Maybe because that's exactly what she'd done.

"Sorry I didn't answer your texts. I didn't see them until this morning. I was too busy with this guy." He nodded toward Hudson, who was drawing across his high chair tray with a finger full of pureed baby food.

"Oh, it's fine. No problem." *Only shaved a year off my life.* Emma pulled out a chair and sank into it. What had she thought would happen? Of course Gage and Hudson would be okay. This morning all of her panic felt silly, but ten hours ago she'd been tormented by what might be occurring over here.

"And in answer to your apology text, you don't have any reason to feel bad. Enough of that."

Except for the fact that she'd coerced him into going out. "So did Hudson calm down on the way home last night?"

"Ah, no. Took him a while to settle, but he did eventually."

"How'd you get him to stop crying?"

"I gave up." Gage spooned another bite into Hudson's open mouth. "I tried everything and nothing worked, so eventually I just held him and let him cry."

Emotion clogged her throat. "And you said you didn't know what you were doing."

"I don't, crazy woman."

"Sounds like the perfect answer to me."

"For some reason you're completely biased and think I can do all things when it comes to Hudson." His shoulder nudged into hers. "I'm not sure where you came up with that theory, but it definitely hasn't been proven."

Disappointingly, his phone rang, interrupting the touch that wouldn't have lasted anyway.

Gage set the spoon and baby food down on the tray and rose, and Emma seized them both before Hudson could make a mess of it. He answered his phone while Emma took over feeding Hudson.

"I'm sorry you cried so much last night, kiddo. That breaks my heart." Hudson stared at her in answer, then broke into a camera-worthy grin. "Well, aren't you in a good mood this morning?"

Gage had walked down the hall to take the phone call, but Emma could overhear him talking. "That's too bad. Sounds like they would have been a good fit… I understand…okay, thanks… I appreciate it."

He returned to the kitchen, the phone in his palm. What had that been about?

"I need to get going if you're okay finishing up with Hudson. Ford's waiting for me."

"Of course. Sorry I was late this morning. I… There was this dream…and then the emergency room." Gage's face contorted with confusion, as it should. *Pull yourself together, girl.* "I overslept." *There you go with the forming of words, Emma! Well done.*

Gage's hands landed on her shoulders. He bent so that she couldn't get away from his piercing stare. Not that she wanted to. "Don't you dare apologize. You've already done so much for Hudson and for me that I can't ever thank you enough. Got it?"

Emma swallowed. Nodded. Inhaled. Did he realize how good he smelled? She wanted to tell him that, no, she hadn't "got it" yet, and could he stay right where he was and convince her some more?

Gage backed up, his hands falling away. Probably a good thing since Emma wasn't here to entertain a crush on the man. She was here for Hudson. In the hopes that he would change Gage's life and vice versa. The two of them were meant for each other.

"So that was Ford on the phone? I didn't mean to over-hear, but…" *I've turned into a nosy shrew, so I figured I'd just ask straight out.*

"It was Rita. We've been keeping in touch, hoping to find a home for Hudson. She put out some feelers to ex-tended family, even friends. A couple from Rita's church was looking to adopt so we thought they might be a match for Hudson, but they just found out they're pregnant and said it's not the right timing for them. Really stinks that they said no. It would be nice if I could quit taking ad-vantage of you and find the right family for Hudson."

A fire lit inside of her. "Don't *you* dare say *that*. Watch-ing Hudson is exactly where I want to be right now. I'm not put out or upset. I love spending time with him."

A smile tugged on Gage's lips, his hands lifting in defense. "Okay."

"You're really great with Hudson. You're loving him well and doing an amazing job with him. I hope you know that." How could Gage continue to consider giving Hudson up? Didn't he know that he was already falling for the boy? The winds—or maybe breezes—of change were beginning to blow, and yet Gage was still work-ing on his plan to find another home for Hudson. Why couldn't he see that he was the right choice?

Gage snorted. "I don't think *amazing* is the right word. Surviving is one thing, but thriving is another. Last night just confirmed that I'm not the right fit for this. For Hud-son. Guess I have you to thank for that."

Emma's mouth dropped open. *No-no-no.* "But… but…" But he'd handled it! Things had turned out fine!

She needed to correct Gage, only his declaration and the fact that he'd given her credit had rendered her speechless.

"Rita did say she'll keep trying, so that's great. It's a setback, but it's not the end of the world. With how much I've been praying for the right match for Hudson, it's good to know without a doubt this wasn't it."

Gage's phone dinged and he checked it. "It's Ford. I'd better go." He slid it into his back pocket, put on his coat and boots, then exited the house after a quick goodbye.

"But what if *this* is the right home?" Sure. Now Emma could speak. Not that Gage wanted to hear what she had to say. The man didn't have any doubts about finding another family for Hudson. But how could he ignore what was right in front of him?

"Da." Hudson added a new sound to his repertoire, almost as if he was attempting to answer Emma's forlorn question. Then he knocked the spoon out of her hand, sending the remaining food flying as moisture pricked her eyes.

"I messed that up, didn't I? And I don't have anyone to blame but my pushy self."

Hudson sucked on his fingers, making a smacking sound.

"But I still think this is the right place for you even if Gage doesn't see it yet."

The baby dragged his fingertips through the food splattered across his tray, then reached out as if offering some to Emma.

"I think I'll get my own breakfast, Sir Hudson, but thank you for the offer." She mock bowed. He chortled.

Emma joined him. How could Gage not see how much life Hudson brought into his world? How was he willing to give that up? *Gage Frasier, I'm nowhere near done with you, and Hudson isn't, either.*

So what if last night had been a temporary setback? It wasn't anything that couldn't be fixed. And since that family had just said no, that gave Emma more time.

Time for Hudson to work his way into Gage's heart, and time for Emma to sit back, pray and watch.

Chapter Six

Gage owed Emma approximately one million dollars, and the ticker was still running. On top of all she usually did for Hudson and him, she'd insisted on staying with the baby tonight while Gage met with Pastor Higgin.

What was supposed to have been a short dinner meeting regarding some land the church was interested in buying had morphed into two-plus hours. Gage's expertise was in contract law, so he wasn't sure how much of a help he'd been. Still, more often than not, he was able to give some insight. And Pastor Higgin had needed to process before he discussed the purchase further with the elders. Gage had been happy to lend a listening ear.

When Emma had caught wind of Gage's plan to find a sitter for the night, she'd protested big-time, touting that Hudson needed consistency right now. How could he debate that? Plus, arguing with Emma when she dug in was like quarreling with a tough-as-nails trial attorney.

She didn't get angry. Didn't yell. She was calm and logical and convincing, and had claimed victory before he'd even formed a rebuttal.

He backed his Grand Cherokee out of Pastor Higgin's

driveway, the homemade desserts Mrs. Higgin had sent with him riding shotgun on the passenger seat.

When he turned into the ranch drive, it was eight thirty. Hudson was likely in bed already, so Gage let himself in quietly.

Emma was sitting on the couch. Her feet—sporting striped socks—were propped on the coffee table. She had a small bound notebook perched in her lap. At his greeting, she plunked her pencil inside, snapped it shut and dropped it onto the coffee table like a hot potato.

"Hey." A bright, commercial-worthy smile flashed, but Gage's attention stuck on the notebook. Or was it a journal? What did those pages contain? And why the quick shutdown?

He hung up his coat and removed his boots. "Brought you something." He delivered the paper plate, clear cellophane wrap leaving the chocolate caramels visible.

Emma's eyes rounded with delight as she accepted the desserts. "Bless Mrs. Higgin. These are my favorites." She lifted the cover and breathed in the contents.

"You're supposed to eat them."

"Ha." Her eyes twinkled, and his nervous system lurched to a grinding halt. Emma was stunning. A thought that had plagued him consistently over the last few days.

Somehow Emma's outward beauty had snuck up on him over time. Perhaps he'd been in a fog the last year or two, and seeing her heart in action with Hudson—and him—had startled him awake. Or he was just an imbecile. Either way, noticing Emma had taken over at least 80 percent of his brain capacity.

He'd morphed into a broken printer, his thoughts spitting out phrases like *Emma pretty*. To which he'd begun silently replying, *Emma off-limits*.

Gage sat in the recliner. "Sorry I kept you out so late."

"I'm good. I didn't have anywhere else to be." Emma put a pillow between her back and the armrest of the couch, extending her legs across the cushions.

"How'd Hudson do tonight?"

"Perfect. He's sleeping now."

"Not that you're biased or anything."

Curved lips registered like a left hook. "Exactly. How was the meeting?"

"Good. Long. But if it helped in some way then it was worth it."

"You're a good man, Gage Frasier." The skin around her eyes crinkled, respect and appreciation radiating. Had anyone ever looked at him the way Emma did? Even in friendship, he could tell how much she cared about him. Gage had thought when he'd met Nicole that they were perfect for each other. But over time, her outward beauty had diminished, and he'd come to the wretched realization that at the core, she was self-focused. It had been too late to change anything at that point. They were married, and he'd committed.

Only that word had carried a different definition for Nicole.

"I'm just trying to be as giving as you are, Emma Wilder."

Amusement danced across her features. "That's crazy talk." She plucked a caramel from the plate and took a bite, then swallowed while releasing a hum of contentment and appreciation. "I have a deep and abiding affection for Mrs. Higgin. She's so kind and wise and wonderful. But currently my love for her is based solely on the fact that she sent these home with you." Emma finished the treat and brushed unseen crumbs from her fingertips. "The only thing that could possibly make them any better is a cup of tea to accompany them."

"I'll make you one." Gage popped up.

"What? No. I'm leaving. I don't need to keep you."

Keep him? What did Gage have to do at night but fit in some contract work for his old firm or read about ranching—market conditions, water sources, how to save time and money with swath grazing. Riveting stuff.

"Stay for a few minutes?" Man, he was greedy when it came to Emma's time. She'd made dinner a few nights recently and stayed to eat with him and Hudson. It had been the bright spot in his day. Gage had gotten used to having Emma around in the evening, and he liked it. He'd missed out on that tonight because of dinner with Pastor Higgin and his wife.

Emma's mouth softened. "Okay."

"Although one of these days I'm going to convince you that you're missing out on coffee. *That* would be amazing with one of those."

"I'll take your word for it."

"Sure you don't want me to make you some decaf?"

"You're as pushy as Mackenzie when it comes to that bitter stuff."

Gage got out the box of teas he'd ordered for Emma and heated the water—no kettle at his house, so the microwave would have to do.

"Since when do you know how to make tea, Counselor? I thought you were strictly a macho coffee man."

Counselor. The name rolled off Emma's tongue as if she'd used it before. She hadn't—at least, not around him. But he liked the sound of it coming from her.

"I learned from observing you." He glanced over his shoulder. She was still in the same spot, amusement and maybe a bit of contentment evident as she watched him. About time he could do something for her, even if it was just making a simple cup of tea.

He questioned which kind she wanted, then added the tea bag to the water and delivered her mug.

"Thanks." She palmed the cup and must have decided it was too hot because she quickly switched to the handle. "Nothing for you?"

"Nope. Mrs. Higgin fed me way too much. And I may have eaten more than my share of those." He nodded toward the desserts as he reclaimed the recliner.

"Not that it shows on you." Emma's eyes flew wide after her comment, and his grin sprouted. Emma was welcome to say nice things about him anytime.

"Right back at ya."

"Oh, please." She waved a hand, dismissing his comment. "I've always been a medium and that's what I'll always be."

"What's that mean? Are we talking sizes?"

Emma groaned. "Did I just say that out loud?"

"Yep."

She picked a fuzz from the couch, seemingly finding the process quite intriguing. "Well," she looked up, "since I can't seem to keep my mouth shut, it means a few things. On a good day, medium is my size." Her teeth pressed into her lower lip, tugging it endearingly to one side. "Not that you needed to know that," she added, her cheeks turning pink. "But it also refers to me in general. I grew up with twin siblings who were larger than life. Still are. Kenzie's adventurous and Luc's always tried his own thing when the mood strikes. I don't take big risks or want a lot more than I have. I like my life. I'm the meek little sister. Not interesting enough to be small or petite and have that daintiness going for me. Not long and willowy like Mackenzie. Medium through and through."

Emma's theory was completely unfounded. She was the most amazing person. Sweet and kind and funny and distractingly pretty. "I wouldn't use *meek* or *medium* to describe you."

"Really?"

"Nope. And willow trees are overrated."

She laughed, then beamed, and his skin warmed under the glow. "Thanks."

"I'd say you're more like…sunshine." And not the crisp winter kind. The warm summer kind that filtered through the leaves of trees and spoke of swimming pools and forts and long, lazy days. "You're irresistible. That's why everyone wants to be around you."

Moisture glistened, making her intriguing eyes shimmer. "That might be the nicest thing anyone has ever said to me."

"People are fools not to see you for who you are, Emma."

"Oh my!" She fanned her neck. "All of these compliments are making me overheat."

A chuckle rumbled in his chest. "So, what did you do tonight after Hudson went to sleep?" His eyes bounced off the notebook on the coffee table. Would she tell him what was in there? Or was it too private?

"I was working on some ideas for the ranch."

"Mine or yours?"

"Wilder." The word tumbled out with a hint of laughter.

"Kids' Club stuff? I would assume this is the time of year you normally prep for the summer. How are you handling all of that while watching Hudson?" And why hadn't Gage thought to ask her that question previously? Probably because he'd assumed he wouldn't have Hudson living with him for very long.

"Oh, I'm working some at night and while Hudson naps when I'm here. Right now it's just about hiring summer staff and developing this year's program and theme. Since so many families come back year after year, I like to change things up for the kids. But that's not what I was thinking about tonight."

She sipped her tea.

He waited.

"You really want to know?"

"I do."

"Okay." Her exhale wobbled. Was she nervous to tell him? Why? "I've been thinking of things we could add to the guest ranch experience." She plunked her mug down on the coffee table and then flipped the notebook open. After a few seconds—gathering courage?—she turned it so he could see. The paper contained a few sketches. One of an older building turned into a rustic ice cream parlor, the next a small store.

"So you're an artist on top of all of your many impressive qualities."

"Not a good one. But I have always sketched my ideas. When I was little, I told my dad that we should build a castle lodge. He still has my drawing of it. There may have been a few white stallions and unicorns grazing nearby." Her cheeks creased. "I'm definitely more starry-eyed than I am practical. I'm always dreaming about what we could do to make staying at a guest ranch more tempting in a world where people want every convenience at their fingertips."

"Envisioning how to improve the ranch is a good

thing." And attractive. Intriguing to know there was more to Emma than met the eye. In the past Gage's longer interactions had typically been with Luc. He'd been missing out. "So will you tell Luc and Mackenzie about your ideas?"

"They aren't really looking for this kind of stuff from me. They're usually the big-picture people, and I'm just…"

"Brilliant? Smart? A total asset? I'm not sure which word to fill in, but they all fit."

Emma dropped the notebook onto the couch, momentarily covering her face with her hands. "Stop it. I'm none of those things. Luc teases me that I'm a romantic, and it's true. I come up with lofty ideas that aren't necessarily feasible."

"But aren't there two outbuildings currently not being used that would be a fit for both of those?" He pointed to her drawing.

"Yeah. That's what made me think of it, actually. The ice cream parlor would be a great place for families to hang out in the evenings. And the store idea would be so fun. We could pull in different Colorado handmade goods. Souvenirs with the ranch logo Cate just redesigned. It would be perfect for guests who love to shop. Or to purchase supplies if they've forgotten something for their trip."

"Those are great suggestions, Emma. You should say something to your siblings."

Those distracting lips of hers pressed tightly together. She flipped the journal cover closed, hiding her creativity. "Maybe."

"That sounded more like a no."

"Can I have another one of these?" She motioned to the chocolates, which she'd set on the coffee table earlier.

"Of course. They're for you."

She plucked one from the plate. "I'll think about what you said."

"Are you just saying that so that I'll stop bugging you about it?" He quoted her from the night of the talent show.

An Emma-sweetened, done-with-this-conversation smile answered him.

Gage raised his hands in defeat. "I'll let it go." Only... he didn't understand her reasoning for not saying something. Emma was obviously talented at running the Kids' Club program, but her skills went beyond that, too. Did her siblings see that? Or were their noses buried in the sand? Because Gage suddenly felt quite protective of the woman in front of him who would do anything for anyone else.

Who took care of her?

Emma wasn't used to being so...noticed. It wasn't as though Luc and Mackenzie didn't appreciate her—they did. But with Gage it felt...different.

Better.

She shouldn't have shown Gage her brainstorming sketches. The concepts were silly. Fanciful. But the man had a way of pulling information out of her.

And despite Gage's praise, Emma didn't plan to share the concepts with Luc or Mackenzie anytime soon.

Her siblings had too much going on. Luc and Cate's twins were due in July—smack-dab in the middle of their busiest season—so her brother was working to accomplish whatever he could ahead of time. Mackenzie was video-interviewing staff left and right.

Neither of them had time for anything more right now.

And Emma was quite occupied with Hudson, so she didn't have the capacity to pursue developing a project, either.

Letting the ideas simmer made sense. And if the concepts never came to fruition, that would be fine. Who knew if her daydreams were actually any good? Just because Gage had said so didn't make it true.

Between her watching Hudson and the dinners they'd shared together lately, he probably felt like he owed her.

He didn't. Especially not if he'd actually consider keeping Hudson.

After the talent show fiasco, Gage had once again stuck to home in the evenings. Emma had cooked dinner and stayed to eat with him and Hudson a few nights, hoping to remind him he could have some semblance of normalcy while raising a baby. Wanting to provide some adult companionship so that he didn't drown in isolation.

At first Gage had balked. He'd demanded that she stop doing so much for him and Hudson. He'd tried sending her home. Kicking her out.

But after one meal, his protests had faded.

Over the course of their dinners together, Emma and Gage had gotten closer, and the idea of him raising Hudson had wormed even further into her heart. Gage was gentle and sweet with the boy, the awkwardness that had first plagued their relationship fading with time. Hudson was opening Gage up, softening him.

Yet each day, Emma feared that Gage would walk down the hallway or through the front door and announce to her that he'd found a home for Hudson. And then all of her plans to heal Gage by convincing him to keep Hudson would crumble.

"Anything new with finding a family for Hudson?"

Rows burrowed across his forehead. "Nope." Disappointment weighted down the word.

Gage had nosed into her business tonight, so she felt liberated to do the same. "Can I ask you something?"

"Sure."

"Why are you so certain another home is the right answer? How do you know?"

Gage rubbed the back of his neck. "My childhood growing up was pretty…perfect. My sister and I got along for the most part. We had amazing parents who loved us and enjoyed being with us. They never missed one of our activities. I still have a good relationship with them."

"That's great." Emma sipped her lemongrass tea, which somehow tasted better when Gage made it for her. Was that possible? Of course the image of Gage in the kitchen prepping tea for her certainly didn't hurt anything.

"Exactly. I look back on my childhood and think, I want that for Hudson. A mom and a dad who love each other, who can't get enough of their kids. A whole family unit, not just—" he motioned to himself "—me. And I can't imagine getting married again," his nose wrinkled, broadcasting inner turmoil, "when things went bad with Nicole…"

She inched forward, all ears. Gage didn't talk about Nicole much. Emma knew pieces of what had happened, but there were a lot of blanks.

"It turned ugly. I tried so hard to keep Nicole. To change her into thinking our marriage was where she wanted to be. But it wasn't. Maybe even from the start.

She cheated on me when we lived in Denver. It was an emotional affair the first time around—or so she said—but that didn't lessen the bite."

How could Nicole have done that? Two affairs? How had the woman not seen Gage for the prize he was? "I'm so sorry, Gage. You deserve better than that." *An adoring wife. A brood of children. Someone who appreciates you like...* Emma didn't allow herself to finish the wayward thought.

His eyes crinkled yet remained sad. "Thanks."

"So then what happened?"

"Then we moved here. I hoped completely uprooting our lives would change things. That maybe it was my fault for working too much. For not loving her enough." Gage swallowed, and Emma's heart broke a little. Only Gage would put all of the blame on himself when Nicole had so obviously not made any effort.

"I thought that here, of all places, she would be focused on us and our marriage. As if moving to the ranch would limit her straying. I forgave her for the affair. I thought... I don't know. That's what I was supposed to do. That saving our marriage was worth it."

"Maybe it would have been..."

"If she'd changed." Gage filled in the rest. "But she didn't. She was still the same woman. And she took off at the first opportunity. I threw myself at her feet, attempting to let go of the way she'd wounded me and our marriage in order to save it and us, and she just tossed it all back in my face."

"You fighting for your relationship through all of that gives me hope that there are good men left in the world who love wholeheartedly. Who don't give up, even when things are incredibly hard. I think what you did, the way

you loved her... It was beautiful. Even if it wasn't re-
ciprocated."

Gage blinked, lost somewhere in painful memories.
The agony radiating from him was palpable. It took everything in Emma not to walk over, sit on the arm of his
chair and wrap him in a hug.

"My divorce felt like such an overwhelming failure.
I'm not sure you can understand how awful, how crushing and disappointing it was to lose my marriage after
fighting so hard to keep it."

"Failure is suffocating. I get that."

Gage's head tilted, narrowed eyes questioning. "I can't
imagine that you do, but okay."

*Oh, honey. You have no idea the kind of failing I've
succeeded at.* Emma's situation with James read like a
stilted children's book.

Emma meets guy.

Emma is flattered by the attention from said guy.

Guy is slime.

*Mortified by her choice in men, Emma flees. But her
shame and embarrassment stay with her, because those
are hers alone.*

Just like the choice to get involved with James in the
first place.

He'd told her she was beautiful. That he thought about
her all of the time. That he'd never met anyone like her
before. Emma's romantic heart had fluttered like but-
terfly wings at James's compliments.

They'd dated for about a month. During that time,
he would bounce from a praise to a recommendation.
Something she could or should change about herself.

Her hair or clothes. Toning down her laugh.

Hurtful things.

And then, quick as a whip, he'd be back to waxing on about how amazing she was. He'd confused her. Flattered her. And the worst part was, she'd stuck around for it all a bit too long. During the time they'd dated, James had spun her head in so many directions she'd forgotten which way was up.

Then one morning, she'd been knee-deep in her devotions, and God had opened her eyes to all of the reasons she should be running from James instead of to him. The conviction had been so strong that she'd broken things off…and uncovered a spiteful, malicious side to him she was only too happy to escape. Not long after, James had begun an affair with Nicole and the two of them had left town together.

The whole thing made Emma feel filthy, like she'd been wading through mud puddles and fallen flat on her face while the whole world watched.

"I care about Hudson so much." Gage continued. "But I can't picture myself having kids or providing that kind of family for him. I just…don't have enough confidence in relationships anymore."

So Gage had wanted children before things went bad with Nicole? Heartbreaking.

"I don't have enough faith is what it comes down to."

"In God?"

"No. In me. In my ability to make a marriage work. In my ability to trust someone again." The last thing was said quietly, burdened with a sadness Emma wasn't sure Gage even recognized.

Her chest ached like an elephant had plopped down on it.

"That childhood I told you about with a loving mom *and* dad? I want that for him. Is that so wrong?"

Her heart shattered, the hope she'd harbored over Gage keeping Hudson crumbling with the weight of his admission. "No." Her vocal cords squeaked. "It's not wrong to want that for Hudson."

Gage's reasoning was almost…sacrificial. Giving up Hudson wouldn't be easy for him—Emma could tell that he loved the boy. And yet, he would, for what he believed to be Hudson's sake.

Emma had previously thought that she—or, rather, Hudson—could change Gage's mind. But she'd only been going up against him not wanting kids. She hadn't realized how Gage felt about marriage…that he didn't trust himself or anyone else. So now, in order for Gage to keep Hudson, not only would she have to reverse his thinking about having children, but also about marriage. He'd have to stop believing that the world was full of Nicoles and start believing that he could have a loving, lasting relationship with the right person.

And even with her optimism, Emma didn't know how she'd go about doing that.

Chapter Seven

Hudson and Gage sat in the back row of the church on Sunday morning. Emma was with her family halfway up on the right side, in seats they used so frequently their names could practically be etched into the back of the old mahogany pew.

Gage felt strangely misplaced not sitting with them. Something about Emma pulled him in. Made him feel at home. Like he belonged. And he hadn't felt that way in a long time. Since even before Nicole took off.

It wasn't until partway through the closing prayer that Gage realized he was staring at Emma's back, grinning like a besotted fool at the way she bobbed her head in agreement with Pastor Higgin's requests to God.

A quick glance to his left and right told him his blatant study of Emma had gone unnoticed. Gage slammed his lids closed for the remainder of the prayer.

Hudson climbed up and down in his lap, ready to be released from sitting still. Certainly the boy would much rather be crawling and playing, but when Gage had attempted to leave him in the nursery, Hudson had clung to him. His eyes had welled with tears, and his chubby fist had grasped the buttons on Gage's evergreen shirt like they were his saving grace.

With Zeke's death so fresh and Hudson's life in such upheaval, Gage had quickly caved to keeping the baby with him for the service. Though he'd been so occupied with entertaining and feeding Hudson he hadn't heard much of the sermon at all.

"Amen." Pastor Higgin ended the prayer, and Hudson punctuated it with a burp that must have been jarred loose during his recent movements.

The sound elicited quiet laughter from Gage and some of the other parents near him.

Parents. He sat in a section full of them, and yet he didn't belong. Zeke should be the one holding Hudson. The one raising him, teaching him.

It shattered Gage that not only would Zeke miss out on seeing each new milestone from Hudson, but that the boy would never have the chance to know his amazing father.

If he let himself think too much about any of it, Gage could barely stay upright.

Yesterday Gage had found out that a distant relative of Rita's might be interested in raising Hudson. The Franks were missionaries in Ghana and wanted to discuss things more with Gage when they returned to the States at the end of February. They had three kids already but desired to have more and their doctor had advised that Noreen not carry another pregnancy. The situation sounded promising—like maybe Hudson would be as much of a gift to them as they would be to him. Their visit was still a couple of weeks away, so in the meantime Gage would wait and pray.

The congregation filed into the church meeting hall, where cookies and coffee were being served in celebration of the Grammars' wedding anniversary. Fifty years. What an accomplishment. Gage's parents had just celebrated their thirty-fourth this year. It was amazing how thoroughly he'd botched his own marriage with them as an example.

But then, he often wondered if he and Nicole had been doomed from the start. He'd been instantly taken with her outward beauty and what he'd thought was a great personality. But as time had passed, Gage had begun to wonder if Nicole had used him as a way to escape her dysfunctional family. Had the woman ever really loved him? He'd probably never know.

Emma stepped into the room and scanned, eyes lighting up when they landed on Hudson. Her hair was pulled into a bun today. Small hoops—likely because of Hudson—in her ears. She wore cowboy boots with a jean dress that belted at the waist. Gage's mouth went dry. She was adorable and completely oblivious to the fact, which only made her more so.

In a few steps, she was in front of them. "There's my boy." Hudson lunged into her arms, and she squeezed him tight. "I missed you, Sir Hudson."

If Hudson could talk, he'd no doubt agree to missing Emma. Anytime she wasn't at the house, he peered around every corner as if she might suddenly appear. Gage did, too. Everything was just…better with her around.

Her dancing eyes met his. "How'd last night go?"

"Really good. He slept all the way through without waking up."

"Such a big boy!" She nibbled on Hudson's cheeks. "Good job, buddy." The baby's hand went up, exploring

Emma's face. She switched to hand kisses, the act and Emma's lips driving Gage to distraction.

"What are you up to this afternoon?" She turned her attention from Hudson to him again, and Gage ripped his eyes away from their momentary resting place.

"Not much. The usual." Sundays with Hudson were about survival. Playing with him. Keeping him happy. Emma had at least spent Sundays on her own since Hudson's arrival, but other than that, her presence at his ranch had been consistent. Just how he liked it, surprisingly. "What about you?"

"I have a hot date." A megagrin flashed on her face, practically blinding him, and unexpected jealousy rose up, filling Gage's throat with sand.

His next words barely catalogued above a croak. "Oh, really?"

"Yep. With a new book."

Relief turned his limbs into the slept-for-hours-and-just-woke-up variety. And he really didn't want to delve into discovering why. He'd just chalk it up to being protective of Emma. She was too kind, too sweet for her own good, and the world was full of guys who would happily take advantage of her. But Emma was also smart as a whip. Gage should be more confident that she could handle herself since he'd witnessed her intelligence and fierce determination firsthand.

"My favorite author's newest release arrived on my step last night, and in an act of sheer willpower, I managed to not start reading it." Emma shifted Hudson so that he faced forward. "Because I wouldn't have been able to stop if I had. I'd have been awake until one or two."

"I was up until midnight last night."

"Maybe you were the one with the hot date." Her voice

dipped low along with a sassy tip of her chin. "You holding out on me, Counselor?"

Not a chance. Gage spent all of his time with Emma and Hudson. And cowboys and cattle.

"Not that you have to tell me if you did." A pucker nestled between her eyebrows. "I mean, it's really none of my business."

If he were to go on a date, would Emma care? Because the image of her with someone else made his gut churn like he was trying to digest rocks.

"There's nothing interesting to tell. Just a late-night session with some contracts I've been helping my old firm with. Captivating stuff."

Her face brightened. "Oh! I didn't realize you were working for them still."

"Only when they're swamped. It's good side work, and not to make myself sound like a complete bore, but… I really enjoy it."

She laughed. The sound warmed his body, and he decided right then and there to add *make Emma laugh as much as possible* to his life goals. "You have a great laugh." He hadn't planned to say anything of the sort, but immediately forgave himself for the slipup when Emma's head tilted and a shy curve creased her cheeks.

"Really? I always think it's kind of…loud."

"Who told you that?"

A sad smile surfaced. "It doesn't matter."

Based on her tone and expression, Gage would guess it was a guy who'd said something like that to Emma. A complete moron.

"He was wrong, Emma."

She blinked quickly, and the corners of her mouth quirked. "Thank you." Her quiet response resonated in his chest. He wanted to transport them away from church—out of the sight of any gossipmongers—and tug Emma close. Hold on until she realized just how amazing she was.

A flash of awareness bounced between them, a pinball that couldn't or wouldn't settle into obedience.

"Hey, man." Luc joined them, greeting Gage with a slap on the back, his presence swallowing the previous moment.

A good thing since Emma was a *friend* who was doing a massive favor for him and Hudson. Exactly why she was too good for the likes of Gage. Someday someone would come along and recognize Emma for the treasure she was. Just because Gage could see that now didn't make them right for each other.

Hudson fussed, and Emma bounced gently in answer. He added a kick of annoyance and a squawk. "I'm going to walk around with him while you two discuss boy things." And then she was off. She stopped to talk to some women who cooed over Hudson, eliciting smiles, at home with a baby in her arms.

Gage switched his attention to Luc only to find him watching his sister.

"Why does she look so content?" Luc asked.

"Because she's Emma."

"And she was born to nurture."

"Pretty much." Gage had only known Emma for a couple of years, but based on everything he'd witnessed, he'd have to agree with Luc's assessment.

"I'm concerned about that."

"The nurturing?"

"No. Not if it was her baby she was showing off like a

new engagement ring. But since you're planning to find a new home for him…"

Silence stretched. Expanded. "You're worried about her getting hurt when he goes."

"Yep." Luc's answer was short and not so sweet. Definitely overprotective brother. With good reason.

"That makes sense. I hadn't thought about how close they were getting or how much time they've been spending together. Or what it would do to her when I find another home for Hudson." But he'd been a fool not to. "I'll deal with it." Somehow.

"We have a group at the ranch next weekend. It's a bunch of pastors and their families. While they're being ministered to with their wives, Emma runs the Kids' Club. She only has responsibilities on Saturday and then Sunday afternoon, but the guests don't leave until Monday morning. She's not exactly needed that day, but…"

"It would be the perfect opportunity for her to gain some space and distance from Hudson."

"Exactly. I know it doesn't make it easy on you, figuring things out with Hudson."

"We'll be fine. It's a good idea."

Audible air rushed from Luc. "Thanks. I'm sorry to ask this of you. If Emma finds out we were conspiring she's going to roast us."

"True. But hopefully the weekend away from Hudson will be just what she needs."

"Amen to that. Emma brings out my protective side."

"Mine, too."

"She's so…"

Mesmerizing. Sweet. Beautiful. "I don't want her to get hurt, either. And I'm sorry I didn't think beyond Hudson's needs. I didn't expect to have him for this long. I thought this would all work out faster, but things are progressing slowly."

"I'm not upset with you in the least. You've been put in a tough position, and Emma really is the perfect fit for helping out with Hudson." Luc could say that another hundred times. "I just want to make sure she doesn't get crushed when it all comes to an end."

Gage, too. Which was why he also planned to keep his growing attraction to her under wraps. Allowing anything to start between them when it could never come to fruition was just plain cruel. For everyone involved.

Their conversation turned to other things, but Gage's mind continued to spin. Emma wasn't going to be pleased with the plan he and Luc had just cooked up, but then again, she didn't get to be in charge of everything when it came to Hudson.

It was for her own good, so she'd just have to adjust.

On Thursday morning, Emma entered Gage's house after a quick knock. They'd become so comfortable with their arrangement that she didn't wait out in the cold for him to let her in anymore.

"Morning," Gage called out. He was parked in front of the sink scrubbing a pan—flirt—and Hudson was in his high chair. The boy banged on his tray, stringing together a long line of babbling sounds in greeting.

"Hello to you, too." Emma approached Hudson and kissed his head, managing to find a spot in his hair devoid of scrambled eggs. "Did any of it make it into your mouth?" He grinned in answer. One particularly stubborn piece of egg stuck to his forehead, defying the laws of gravity.

Emma snagged Hudson's washcloth from the edge of the sink and proceeded to clean him up. Once he was good as new, she removed his bib and plucked him from the seat. She moved him into the living room, surrounding him with a few toys that lit up and made noises when he pressed the various buttons.

After that, she switched to the dishcloth and got to work on wiping down the high chair. In a matter of seconds, Gage stole it from her and took over.

"Emma Wilder, you need to quit doing so much work around here."

She crossed her arms and, despite her current close proximity to Gage, didn't scoot back an inch. "Au contraire. You're the one who needs to quit stealing my job."

"It's not your job. I've told you that countless times. I have a house cleaner that comes every other week, Emma. You're already watching Hudson. Do not make me fire your free help."

"Ha-ha." Her attempt to squash any humor was thwarted when a smile snuck through.

"I'm planning on you not being here Saturday because you have a group this weekend."

That was a quick change of topic. "Right." They'd talked about that earlier in the week.

"Sounds like you have quite a bit to do, so I was thinking you should take off early tomorrow afternoon."

On Friday? But why? Her nose wrinkled. "I'm not doing Kids' Club until Saturday, so—"

"But you've been here so much that I'm sure you're behind and could use the time to catch up on work."

Her mouth flopped open and closed like a fish's. "I—"

"And don't come back until Tuesday. That way you'll have Monday, too."

Emma stepped back as if Gage had physically shoved her, hurt catching in her throat like the beginning of a nasty cold. Was he trying to get rid of her? Because if he was, the man should just say it. No need to skirt around the truth. She could handle it. Or figure out how to. Somehow.

"But what about—"

"You're needed at Wilder Ranch, and Hudson and I have taken plenty of your time in the last few weeks. We'll handle the weekend without you and see you on Tuesday. I've already got things figured out. So take a day off if you don't have work to do. You deserve it." He flashed a crisp smile that didn't create the usual shimmy in her abdomen.

Gage's attempt to make his directives and demands sound positive and upbeat were failing miserably, because all Emma registered was the steel beneath the words. He acted as if he were gifting her a much needed break instead of breaking her heart.

Why hadn't he asked her opinion about any of this?

Unacceptable tears blurred her vision. She blinked numerous times, forcing her careening emotions into submission. This wasn't the time or place for an ugly cry. Those were best had in the comfort of her bed with a stack of emergency books and a box of tissues nearby.

"Okay. That's fine." Just dandy. Hudson yelped from the living room. He'd probably wedged himself somewhere. Thankful for the excuse to escape, Emma fled to rescue him.

Either Gage was done with her, he needed space or it really was just about her having the time to help out with the group this weekend.

None of the three options made her feel any better.

* * *

"You're the worst characters ever. You can't even keep me distracted for five minutes." Emma shut the book in her hands and dropped it onto the couch next to her. A second later, she patted the cover. "It's not you guys. You're my favorites and you know it." Hopefully, the fictional characters in her life weren't offended by her undeserved outburst.

She'd chosen a favorite book tonight, hoping it would keep her mind off Hudson and Gage. But the old-faithful pick hadn't come through.

Emma had gone Friday afternoon, all day Saturday, and now most of Sunday without hearing a peep from Gage. Without knowing how Hudson was doing.

And, by sheer willpower, she hadn't texted him once.

At least she had that going for her. Emma didn't have to be told twice that she wasn't needed. Gage's message had come across loud and clear. Maybe she'd overstayed her welcome and Gage was going to find someone else to watch Hudson. Or maybe it really was about her helping with the pastor's group staying at the ranch this weekend. She had run two Kids' Club sessions on Saturday and another this afternoon. But Emma could do that with her hands tied behind her back.

And tomorrow morning after breakfast the group would pack up. So there was no reason Emma couldn't watch Hudson for the day—except one.

Gage didn't want her there.

How many times did she have to repeat the thought before it would stick?

Maybe it was a good sign that Gage wanted to handle Hudson on his own. Emma *should* be proud of him, but that sentiment hadn't floated to the surface; instead, she'd been wading through worry and hurt.

If she knew what was happening over there, she'd likely be just fine. But the lack of information was killing her slowly. Was Hudson okay? Emma should have installed that baby monitor with the camera she'd once jokingly considered. At least then she wouldn't be about to lose her mind.

A knock sounded on the cabin door. *It's not going to be Gage, so don't get your hopes up.*

When Emma had returned to the cabin tonight, she'd donned her favorite pair of pajamas—colorful and soft and striped. They had momentarily made everything better, as pajamas were apt to do.

Did she need to change for whoever was at the door? "Who is it?"

"It's me—Cate." The very female voice had her shoulders notching down.

"Come in." She popped up from the couch to greet her friend.

If it wasn't Gage—or, more importantly, Hudson—Emma would gladly take Cate.

Her sister-in-law came inside and shut the door behind her. "I know you'd rather I have a deep voice, my name start with G and be holding a baby in my arms, but I'll just have to do for tonight."

Emma laughed. "Am I that transparent?"

Cate's teeth tucked behind her lip in lieu of an answer. "I thought maybe you could use some company."

"You're a smart woman."

Cate gave a mock bow, the move reminiscent of something Ruby would do. "Thank you."

"How long do I get you? Should I make some tea?"

"That would be great if I'm not interrupting you." Cate took off her coat, revealing preppy button-up pajamas—pink-and-red checked—and slide-on slippers with rubber bottoms. Though the jaunt from Luc and Cate's up the hill to the cabin wasn't far at all, Emma was surprised to see Cate had risked wearing pajamas when the ranch had guests. The woman was usually all things put together. But maybe she was just becoming accustomed to ranch life. Relaxing a bit. A good thing if that was the case.

"Are you kidding? I'm delighted to have you all to myself." Cate was welcome to interrupt Emma's hike down worry lane anytime.

"Go sit." Emma waved Cate into the living room and moved to the sink, filling the kettle and setting it on the burner.

"How was today's session?" Cate asked while Emma retrieved the tea.

"Great. The kids were so sweet. We had a good time while the parents were off bettering their minds." Every year Wilder Ranch hosted this same retreat. It was a weekend of supporting pastors and their spouses, and Emma enjoyed that she got to have a few hours of fun with the kids each day while their parents refueled and recharged. "How are you? Luc said you weren't feeling great this morning."

Cate sank to the couch and arranged two pillows behind her back. "I'm good now. I had an upset stomach. Not sure if it was morning sickness or something else." She rubbed her rounding tummy. "I caked on a bunch of essential oils and took a nap. I felt better as the day went on. Thanks for letting Ruby hang with the kids today. I know that's not really the best protocol, but it was just one of those days."

Emma faced Cate and leaned against the counter as she waited for the water to boil. "Ruby is always welcome wherever I am. I love that girl. She told me today that she's going to marry one of the boys in her preschool class. He just doesn't know it yet."

Cate's head shook, laughter spilling out. "Let me guess—Beau, right?"

"Yep. Is he the blond one with those huge blue eyes? His family sits on the left side in church, almost all the way to the back?"

"That's him."

"She has good taste. That is one adorable kid."

"True. Every time she talks about him, Luc tells her she has to be thirty before she can date."

"I may agree with him on that." When the kettle whistled, Emma added the tea bags and water to mugs, then carried them into the living room. She placed both on the coffee table so they could steep and then sank into the chair flanking the couch.

Cate grinned. "And here I thought I was the overprotective one. Is Kenzie still with the group? She sent Luc home a bit ago."

"Yep. She took the late shift for manning the lodge and closing things down tonight. Bless her." Emma had offered to help since there was no Kids' Club after dinner, but Kenzie had sent her back to the cabin claiming she was "of almost no use" today. Emma would be more offended if it wasn't so true. She had been preoccupied by thoughts of Gage and Hudson all weekend long. It was a wonder she hadn't lost a kid on the hay rides or had one get injured from her lack of attention.

"That was nice of her."

"Definitely." And very Mackenzie to handle everything herself.

Cate picked at a piece of lint on her pajama bottoms. "There's a chance I was rather snarky when Luc got home tonight."

"Oh?" Emma pressed her lips together to avoid giving in to a grin. "And why would that be?"

Chagrin danced across her features. "I guess I might be just a titch emotional."

"I suppose being pregnant with twins might do that to a girl."

Cate laughed. "It's possible. Plus, none of my clothes fit and it's making me feel awful. Like I'm a house already, and I'm only in my second trimester. I've been wearing pajamas for days. Or yoga pants. They're all that I can squeeze into lately except for my maternity clothes, which I don't love. I hardly kept anything, but what I do have was way cuter five years ago." Her nose wrinkled. "And I don't feel good when I dress that way. I mean, sometimes it's fine, but I typically…try."

Emma laughed. "Well, if it helps at all, you currently look very cute. Like you've stepped out of the pages of an L.L. Bean catalogue."

Cate's eyes widened. "How did you know that's where my pajamas are from?"

"Ha! I didn't. It was just a guess. And while you are very much rocking them, not fitting into anything stinks. You do know what that means, don't you?"

"What?" Unease crossed her face.

"We must shop."

A smile sprouted. "I can get behind that theory."

"We could go to Denver."

"I'm in. When?"

"I could do a weeknight. Or a Sunday. Or I might have plenty of free time heading my way in the next few days and weeks if Gage has his way." If Gage was intent on replacing her, maybe Emma wouldn't be watching Hudson at all anymore.

"Ah. Did we finally reach the part where you tell me how you're not stressing over not seeing Hudson?"

"I'm not stressing. I'm just…curious. I know it's not the same because Hudson's not my kid, but if you didn't see Ruby for a couple of days and didn't hear any updates, wouldn't that drive you nuts?"

Cate palmed her tea and then settled back against the pillows. "Of course I'd worry. That's normal."

"So then why is Gage punishing me like this?"

"Em, I don't think he's trying to hurt you. He probably just wants to give you some time. Some space. You've become attached to Hudson very quickly."

"And how, exactly, am I supposed to not become attached to him?"

Cate winced. "I have no idea. But what about when Gage finds a family for Hudson? What then?"

She exhaled and repeated Cate's words. "I have no idea."

Silence ate at Emma as Cate sipped her tea, her face contemplative. "I know this isn't easy. Have you been praying about all of this?"

"Yes." And no. Emma had been praying for Hudson quite a bit, but not about her own part in taking care of him. That portion just seemed…natural. Why did she need to petition God about it? Okay, fine. So she was going to be in a world of hurt when Hudson's time with Gage was over. But how could Emma not fall for Hudson? She could tell herself she was only watching him temporarily. Like a true nanny. A babysitter. But it had been more than that from the start for Emma. Hudson and Gage were beginning to feel like family. How was she supposed to change her state of mind?

She could run. Hide. Exactly what Gage had given her the opportunity to do this weekend, and instead, she'd been focused on the baby's well-being the whole time. Wondering how he was. Praying Gage and Hudson were doing well together.

It was too late not to care as deeply as she already did. Was that an ability Emma even possessed?

"I've been praying for you. For all of you."

Emma gave a watery laugh. "Well, that's just going to make me cry." Cate's admission made Emma stumble and pause. She wasn't alone in this. She had her people. And God. Giving up Hudson, even though he wasn't technically *hers*, might be one of the hardest things she'd have to do in her twenty-three years, but God wouldn't leave her to endure it alone.

"I'm worried about you. Concerned that you're going to be crushed when Gage gives up Hudson."

Cate was right to be alarmed on that account. Emma had prayed so hard for Gage to be changed from the inside out so he'd keep Hudson that she hadn't prepared for the opposite.

"I don't know how to *not* love that little boy with everything that I am."

Cate's soft smile answered her. "And that's exactly why we all adore you so much. You give your all with everything you do, Emma. It's why you're so fabulously wonderful that if I didn't like you so much, I'd be jealous of who you are." The curve of her mouth increased.

"You're amazing. God made you with a gigantic heart. But please try to be careful with yourself."

"I'll do my best." That was as close as Emma could get to the truth without admitting to Cate that it was already too late.

From the moment she'd held Hudson—even back when she'd listened to Gage's dilemma of figuring out whether or not to keep him—she'd already been long gone.

Chapter Eight

Hudson was a wreck, and Gage was running a close second in that department. They'd done so well all weekend, and then starting in the middle of Sunday night the boy had woken numerous times to declare that he was crabby and unhappy and generally mad at the world. Nothing Gage did made any difference in his demeanor.

It was unlike previous times when he'd cried or been upset. This was more…disgruntled. Some tears. More complaints.

And everything Gage attempted to do to comfort him was met with a shaking head or a hand that pushed away his offer.

Each time Hudson had woken last night, Gage had tried to feed him a bottle. He'd acted interested but then would quickly change his mind, spitting out the nourishment.

This morning Gage had managed to get a few bites of applesauce in him, but that was it. The fact that Hudson refused to eat had Gage's unease skyrocketing. He might not know much about babies, but that same symptom would concern him with cattle.

Was Hudson sick? Would Gage even know if he was?

He was currently holding Hudson in the recliner. The boy shoved a fist partway into his mouth, stringing together "m" sounds over the intrusion, misery lacing every syllable.

It *almost* sounded like he was asking for Emma. Or maybe that was just the main thought echoing in Gage's mind.

Emma would know what to do. But based on how she'd left his house on Friday afternoon, she wasn't very happy with him.

She hadn't actually *said* anything, but she'd been quiet and moody. Less sunshine, more storm cloud. Hopefully, the weekend had allowed her to add a layer of protection when it came to Hudson. That would at least make the Emma-empty days worth it.

Should Gage call her about Hudson?

The whole reason he'd pushed her away was so she could gain some distance, not be so emotionally involved with the boy. And now he was going to interrupt that?

But if Hudson *was* sick… Emma would never forgive him for not reaching out. At Hudson's arrival, when Emma had fallen asleep in her car, Gage had assured her that he would reach out if they needed her. He'd asked her to trust him in that.

So that left him no choice in the matter.

The phone rang three times before Emma answered. Her hello was casual. She didn't acknowledge it was him, but she had to know based on caller ID. Definitely still nursing a grudge. That was just fine. Emma could kick and scream and rail at him. He'd be okay with that as long as it kept her from being hurt in the long run.

He skipped a greeting in return. "Hudson's not himself. I'm worried something's wrong."

"I'll be right over."

Gage left his phone on the butcher-block island and paced the room with Hudson. "Emma's coming over, okay, bud? Maybe she'll know what you need."

The baby's face contorted, and he let out a whimper in answer. Poor kid.

Emma arrived at his place far faster than she should have. Gage had the door open before she could knock. "Did you speed all the way over here?" Completely dangerous and unnecessary. "I'm not okay with you risking life and limb to save five or ten minutes."

"Hello to you, too." Emma entered the house, shutting the door behind her as she took off her coat, dropping it and her purse onto the floor. Her arms opened and Hudson lunged for her.

The baby released a relieved sigh once he was tucked inside Emma's embrace, and Gage's exhale followed suit. The boulder that had been crushing his chest all morning and half the night crumbled to pieces and crashed to the ground.

Emma might be mad at him, but her arrival was still a warm spring breeze.

"Hey, Sir Hudson." She ran a hand over his head, lips following behind. "What seems to be the matter? Has Gage been reading legal contracts to you?"

"Ha." He gave a dry retort, but a chuckle quickly followed. "Not funny." Except it was.

Emma placed the back of her hand against Hudson's forehead. Then she pressed her lips there and held. "He's warm but not overly. What's he been acting like?"

"Cranky. Unhappy. Doesn't want to eat. Do you think he could be sick?"

"Does he have any symptoms? A runny nose? Fever?"

"Neither of those. Though my attempt to take his temperature in his armpit did not go well." Gage had searched online for how to take a baby's temperature, and then he'd practically ended up in a wrestling match with the boy because Hudson had wanted to shove the thermometer in his mouth and chew on it. "He's been drooling a ton. Won't eat. He woke up a few times last night and fussed but didn't want a bottle. It was more like he just wanted to complain, but I can't figure out what's bugging him."

Emma had been swaying lightly with Hudson tucked against her shoulder while Gage filled her in. Her mouth found the baby's ear, her voice quiet. "What's wrong, sweet boy? I wish you could tell us."

She walked across the living room and back a few times. Gage sat on the couch and prayed, as he had been doing. These were the instances that only confirmed he wasn't the right guardian for Hudson.

If he didn't have Emma to help, what would he do?

Emma paused midstep as if an idea had hit her. She slid a finger into Hudson's mouth. After some exploration, understanding dawned on her features.

"He's teething. Run your finger along his upper gum."

Sure enough, Gage found the interruption on the smooth surface. Barely existent, but about to push through. No wonder the boy was so irritable.

"That's crazy. How am I supposed to know something like that?" If a family would just come through for Hudson, then Gage wouldn't be bumbling along like he was. In the meantime, he should probably start reading baby books so he could figure this stuff out and know what was headed his way.

"You're not, I suppose. There's numbing gel you can put on his gums. And some people use an amber necklace that's supposed to help with teething pain."

Emma was speaking gibberish.

"Oh! I remember my mom telling me that she had a trick that worked great on us kids. I'll call and ask her." She dug her phone out of her purse, found the number and hit Call, all while holding Hudson and making it look easy as pie.

Emma explained things to her mom, then listened. "Okay. That should work. Thanks, Mom. Love you." They disconnected and Emma tossed her phone back into her purse. "She said back in the day they didn't have all of this fancy stuff like we do now. She used to freeze a wet washcloth. Once it was icy, she'd warm up one end of it so we could hold on and leave the rest. I guess we loved to chew on it. And she said in the meantime, anything cold or—"

Midsentence, Emma took off down the hallway.

"Or what?"

No answer. Gage followed, finding her in Hudson's room. "I thought I remembered seeing some other teething things in his stuff." She opened the drawer of the dresser and rummaged through where Gage had deposited all things Hudson that he hadn't known what to do with. "Here we go!" Emma held up a plastic banana that sported a brush at the end. "This looks like the golden ticket."

She handed it to Hudson, who promptly shoved it into his mouth. She rummaged some more, found a small tube of what must be numbing gel, then closed the drawer.

"I think we should put a few things in the freezer. Washcloth. Teething ring. This may not last long, so we should get prepared." She scooted past him. "I saw some of those frozen fruit teething things in his stuff, too. Let's freeze something to go in that for later."

"Sounds good."

In the kitchen, Gage put some strawberries in the freezer along with a teething ring and a wet washcloth. Emma rubbed the gel onto Hudson's gums and he went back to chomping on the toy banana.

"I'm guessing once this kicks in and he gnaws on something cold, he might be ready to eat."

"Good." Relief rolled along Gage's spine.

"Should we put on a movie? Might be a good distraction."

"I tried earlier and it didn't work, but it might now." Especially now that Emma was here.

"What do you think, Hudson?" She carried him into the living room and adjusted his activity saucer so that it was in front of the television. Then she put in one of Hudson's favorite DVDs. Once it began and his interest was piqued, she gently lowered him into the seat.

Emma backed up a step and waited. Then another. Hudson stayed glued to the movie, not even twisting to check on her whereabouts.

"How do you do that?"

Her line of vision switched from Hudson to Gage standing behind the couch. "What do you mean?" She came his direction, stopping in front of him.

"Twenty minutes ago, I wasn't sure how we were going to survive the day, and then you show up, solving and fixing, and suddenly everyone is happy again." Including himself. When Emma had first arrived, Gage hadn't allowed himself to think beyond helping Hudson. But now he drank her in like a first sip of hot coffee on a snowy morning. "I'm really glad you're back."

The toe of her ankle boot tapped as her arms hugged the soft yellow sweater she wore. "Really? Because I was starting to wonder if…" Her head shook. "Why did you send me away this weekend? I could have figured out how to help at the retreat and check on Hudson. And I certainly didn't need to leave early on Friday. But you didn't ask, you just decided without my input."

Emma wasn't steaming as he'd worried she might be. Based on her drooping shoulders and tone, she was lodging closer to sad.

Which was even worse. "You're right. I'm sorry."

Her self-hug tightened. "Are you done with me? Do you want to hire a nanny for Hudson? Because that's fine if you do. It's your decision, I just—"

His snort interrupted her. "Hire someone else? Are you crazy? Besides the fact that you've yet to let me pay you for your time, there is no one as amazing as you, Emma. Of course I don't want anyone else." The "I" hung between them, changing the connotation of what he'd said but not making it untruthful. Gage didn't want anyone but Emma in his house. In his life or Hudson's. This wasn't just about the baby anymore—no matter how many times he told himself it was.

Gage liked having Emma around. Her presence was addicting. Distracting. On more than one occasion Gage had caught himself thinking about what it would be like to kiss Emma. To lean in and taste that adorable lower lip of hers. Kiss away the weekend and his mistakes with an apology that didn't require words.

Emma's hands fell to her sides, and she sucked in a

breath as if he'd said the thought out loud. He was 99 percent sure he hadn't. Hudson was a few feet away from them, but in this moment, it was just the two of them. A current hummed and neither of them spoke. Neither moved.

Reality settled in along with a keen sense of disappointment.

Emma believed in happily-ever-afters and castle lodges and *I do's* that lasted for fifty years. It didn't take a rocket scientist to see that the woman was born to be a mom and wanted to have kids one day.

Despite caring deeply for Hudson, Gage still did not. And, he reminded himself, that wasn't a crime.

"Then why'd you boot me out of here?" A cute pucker claimed Emma's brow.

"A couple of reasons. One, Hudson and I have taken up so much of your time lately, and I didn't want your work to suffer. And two, Luc and I thought that maybe you—"

"My brother?" Emma's quiet, torn response made his chest ache. "What does he have to do with any of this?"

Great. Now not only would Emma be upset with him, but Luc, too.

And Gage was at fault in all of it. For hiding their not-so-smart plan from her and then accidentally spilling the beans. For managing to hurt the woman who'd made the sun shine in his life again. And for wanting her at his side when she was, most definitely, off-limits.

Had Gage and Luc conspired about her? Why? A sluggish beat ricocheted inside Emma's rib cage, as if the pumping blood couldn't swim through her traumatized veins.

Gage groaned and scrubbed a hand across the back of his neck, casting his eyes to the ceiling. "This is all coming out wrong."

Emma counted to five silently, stretching the *Mississippis* out. "Okay. Then figure out how to say it right. I'll wait."

His earnest look almost had her accepting his explanation before he spoke. "Luc and I were both worried about you because of how close you've gotten to Hudson and the fact that I'm not keeping him. We thought that if you had some time away from him, it would help you take a step back. Re-evaluate. You could gain some distance and then not be so wounded when he goes."

So Gage had been trying to protect her, not get rid of her. Emma expected that kind of behavior from Luc. Her older brother had often watched out for her, whether she wanted him to or not. But Gage's involvement was new. And not altogether unwelcome.

Gage worrying about her meant he cared for her, and she was warmed by that. But the way he'd gone about it stunk like stepping in a pile of manure in flip-flops. Which she'd done before. Ew.

"Boys are dumb when they make decisions for a girl without asking."

A bark of laughter escaped from Gage, a slow grin following. "I couldn't agree more."

Emma's lips bowed. This man softened her like melted butter and he didn't even need a heat source.

"I don't know why I didn't just talk to you about it and explain. Definitely not my best move." Gage's baby blues danced with remorse and self-deprecating humor, making her stomach twirl like Ruby in a full skirt. The man would make gorgeous children. Such a pity he didn't plan to have any.

"I understand why you did it." She poked him in the chest—a wall of strength under a long-sleeved button-up shirt. "I'm not saying I agree with your actions, but if you're asking for forgiveness, you have it."

"Good. Because I don't like making you mad."

"I wasn't mad so much as...hurt."

His mouth pursed to the side. "I like that even less. I'm sorry, Em."

He'd called her *Em*. Little cartoon hearts were likely shooting from her eyes and tummy and any other warm, fuzzy places inside of her. The shortened name felt intimate. It only made her want more. Of him. Of Hudson.

Perhaps Gage and Luc had been right to send her off and hope she'd build some walls. Protect herself. But that just wasn't who she was.

"Are you going to be okay when Hudson goes? Because I'm still worried about you. I think you've fallen for him."

He might not be the only one. "I'm definitely smitten with that boy. And I'm quite confident that I'm going to be a mess when you find another home for him. It isn't in my DNA to *not* care deeply. I don't have that switch."

A grin that had her stomach flipping like pancakes surfaced, coupled with a hint of sadness. "That's why you're so lovable. Because you give it so freely."

Lovable but not *loved*. Not by Gage. Not by any other man. Those were two very different things, and one of these days, Emma really wanted to experience the second.

Hudson squawked. He'd thrown his banana teether, so Emma retrieved it for him. She handed it off, made sure he was content again, and returned to Gage. "I thought maybe you'd hired someone else to watch Hudson this weekend."

"No. I worked as much as I could but wasn't much of a help. Ford's been covering for me. We worked in the barn cutting fence stays on Saturday. I bundled Hudson up, and Ford and I rigged up his bouncy swing so that he couldn't collide with anything. The kid went to town."

Emma could just imagine Hudson's delight at that. There really wasn't a great place for him to use it in the house.

Gage was so good with Hudson and he didn't even realize it. It pained Emma to think he was still going to give the boy up. "Sounds like you survived just fine without me. At least until this morning."

"We managed okay." He squeezed her arm, ran a thumb across her bicep. "But Hudson and I don't want to survive without you." His voice swung low, beseeching. "Does that change anything?"

He's referring to you taking care of Hudson. Don't read anything more into it than that. Still, her pulse raced and she melted into liquid caramel. None of which she planned to admit.

"Do you want me to…" Emma didn't complete the offer. She was still raw and tender from the weekend and would be quite thankful to avoid dipping her toes into that pool of torment again.

"Stay? Yes. But I don't want to ask that of you. You were supposed to have the day to yourself."

What did it say about her that she didn't want to be anywhere but here? "I'm happy to take care of Hudson."

Gage remained silent, studying her. "Are you absolutely sure it's not an imposition?"

Actually, staying away from the two of you is becoming the bigger imposition. But let's not discuss trite details like that right now.

"I'm sure."

"Then I'll gratefully accept your help. Hudson could use your comfort today. Everything is better when you're here."

If only her system didn't compute Gage's words and assume they had something to do with her outside of her role as Hudson's caregiver.

"I owe you big-time. Again. Or more like still. I'll grab takeout tonight if you're interested. Your pick."

"You're going to drive into town to pick up dinner?"

"Actually, the Berrets live just past me, and their son Tommy is usually willing to deliver when he's on his way home from work. He likes the addition to his gas fund. But yes, I would drive into town for you."

Do not swoon over that, Emma Wilder. Don't you dare swoon over that. "You take this apology stuff seriously, don't you?"

"I do. If you need me to write one up for you, I will."

Humor simmered, quickly spiking to a boil. "That won't be necessary." Although she wouldn't mind seeing what Gage would come up with. But that was because Emma was eternally optimistic even when she shouldn't be. Gage's apology would be all legalese and no romance-ese. Better to skip it and the disappointment.

"We've missed you over here. Just look how happy Hudson is now that you've returned." He nodded toward the baby, who was attempting to eat the small plastic mirror adhered to his saucer. "I'm afraid if you leave Hudson will start fussing again. We need you."

Need, not *want*. Again, words with two very different meanings.

"Okay, Counselor. I'll stay *and* take you up on dinner—even though your enticement isn't necessary." She sprinkled the words with teasing instead of the sense of loss and yearning that filled her. Her fake perkiness must have worked, because Gage's cheeks creased in answer.

Hudson gave a frustrated cry that quickly escalated. Emma rescued him from the saucer while Gage got the washcloth from the freezer. He ran warm water over one end and brought it to the baby.

"Here, bud. Hold on right here." He offered the warm part to Hudson and the boy seized it.

He gummed the icy portion as if it were dusted in sugar, and Emma wiped a line of drool from the corner of his mouth.

Hold on. Gage's phrase echoed in her mind. That's exactly what she had to figure out how to do with her heart. Because not only was Hudson snatching up serious portions, Gage was buying up real estate, too.

And, unfortunately, unless Gage changed his mind about marriage and kids, he was all wrong for her. Even if he was beginning to feel right.

Chapter Nine

Gage swung the ax into the ice covering the pond that the cattle needed access to for hydration. Earlier this morning it had sleeted, but then the temperature had plummeted and the moisture had switched to snow. White flakes had been spitting from the sky ever since. So much had dumped that he'd driven the snowmobile out here and sent the guys home before heading out to complete this last necessary task.

The crash of the ax meeting ice again and again broke into the quiet, swirling blanket of white as Gage chopped a parallel line about a foot or so from the shoreline.

It had been a long, frigid day of making sure the cattle had provisions, and Gage was chilled to the bone. Ready for his warm house.

And Emma.

And Hudson.

Having the two of them to come home to might not be permanent, but was it so wrong to enjoy their company while it lasted?

If only Gage had met Emma earlier. Before Nicole. Back then he'd wanted it all—a wife and kids. A house full of laughter and warmth. But that picture had turned cold and brittle, and he had as much chance of heating that old dream back to life as he had of melting the ice on the pond in front of him with a single glance.

And since Emma wanted a future that he didn't—she deserved that and more—it was Gage's job to tame his increasing attraction to her. To everything about her.

He rested the ax on solid ground, propped his palms against the handle and scanned the terrain. Miles of hills and crevices led up to defiant mountains that were currently hiding behind low, gray clouds. Out here would be a great place to dig a hole and bury his disruptive Emma fixation. To kick his growing need for her to the curb.

But that wasn't going to happen, was it? Because wiping clean the impact she'd had on him in the past few weeks was impossible.

His grunt of frustration echoed into the quiet, and he lifted the ax for another blow.

Just because the attraction itself wouldn't go away didn't mean Gage couldn't hide it. Toss some frozen ground over it and deny its existence. Because Emma was everything that was good in the world, and Gage refused to hurt her.

At least, not again. Wounding her over the weekend had been awful, and that had just been about him controlling her time with Hudson. Trying to protect her. How much more damage would he cause if he let himself think about Emma in that way? Because eventually, if something did develop between them, it would have a horrible ending. The kind that would burn both of them to the ground.

But laying to rest the hold she had on him was easier said than done. Because the glimpse of his world without

Emma in it over the weekend had been empty. Rudderless. And then yesterday she'd breezed back into their lives. Forgiven Gage for his stupidity—for hurting her. She'd slipped back into their routine as if she'd never been gone.

Hudson had done so much better with her around, and overnight his tooth had broken through. This morning he'd greeted Emma with delight and waving arms.

The woman just made everything better. Lighter. She couldn't help it.

Gage simply could not go anywhere near thinking of Emma as more than a friend—for both of their sakes. But maybe he could admit to himself that he'd missed her this weekend. Like a man missed the ability to see. Or walk. Or breathe.

Surely that small concession had to be acceptable.

He connected his line in the ice to the shore on both ends, then began chopping a divider every few feet. He returned the ax to the back of the refurbished snowmobile, trading it for the shovel. Scooping up the chunks of ice he'd cut free, he tossed them to the bank behind him. Gage continued down the line until he had a long, wide berth cleared.

After securing his supplies to the snowmobile, he headed for shelter. The wind bullied him on the drive back, whipping snow and decreasing visibility. The weather was deteriorating by the minute.

Gage stored the machine in the barn and then trekked across to the house. A gust pushed him from behind as he twisted the knob, and the door swung open with such strength that he practically fell inside. He latched it quickly to keep out the bitter temperatures.

No sign of Emma in the living room or kitchen, but

the house smelled amazing, so she must be cooking something. A longing that Gage was certain he'd suppressed years ago rose up inside of him.

Would it be so wrong to want this? A second chance? A family to come home to at the end of the day?

But therein lay the problem. Emma and Hudson weren't his to keep. And fairy-tale endings were better left in books or movies. Fitting for Ruby. Or Emma.

That garnered a grin.

Gage stowed his things so they could dry and then made his way down the hallway. Emma's voice came from Hudson's room, and he paused in the doorway.

She didn't turn. Must not have sensed him. She was too busy throwing Hudson into the air. The movement tugged her striped shirt away from her wrists. With an army-green sleeveless vest over it, battered jeans and cowboy boots, her hair flying back as she tipped her head, Emma was mind-numbingly pretty.

"Who's the yummiest boy?" Emma caught Hudson, stretching his deep brown footie pajamas tight as she layered numerous smooches to his face. "Who's the yummiest boy in the whole world?" More flying and kisses. Hudson belly laughed. She nibbled on both of his cheeks, peppering him with those generous lips. Gage could safely say he'd never wanted to be the yummiest boy before.

Mind changed.

Emma caught Hudson again, and Gage forced himself to speak. "Hey."

Her head swung to him, those amazing steel-blue eyes widening with relief. "Oh, I'm so glad you're back."

Her sweet, welcoming response rendered his throat dry as a Colorado drought. And then she crossed the space and enveloped him in an Emma-Hudson hug. The portion of his hair that hadn't been protected by his hat was wet from the snow and his face temperature probably resided somewhere near ice-cube level, but Emma didn't retreat. Hudson fisted his hair in greeting, and between the two of them, the day's stress vanished into thin air.

Gage tightened his arms around them. A friendly hug wasn't breaking the rules, was it?

"Thank you, Emma."

"For what?" Her voice was muffled against his shirt.

"For changing Hudson's life. For making this ranch into a real home for him, even if it is temporary."

Her arms tightened in answer.

When Uncle Kip had left Gage the ranch, he'd also left a monetary inheritance for his sister. The man had probably only spent a small portion of what he'd made over the years.

Neither of them had ever expected to inherit what they'd received. The ranch had been an answer to a prayer Gage hadn't even known to utter. It had provided a chance to start over with Nicole. And after that attempt hadn't worked, it had become a place to pour himself into. To dive into learning something new. Even working his body to the bone with physical labor had been a blessing because it had allowed him to fall into bed at night and sleep soundly.

And now that Emma and Hudson were here, the ranch was starting to feel like a true home. What would Gage do when his prayers were answered and the right family came along for Hudson?

He'd be as much of a mess as Emma had admitted she

would be. But for the baby's sake, and for Zeke, Gage would do what was best for Hudson.

Emma let go and stepped back, and Gage fought the temptation to pull them both close again.

"I heard the guys take off a bit ago and then assumed you'd be in shortly. The weather has been so nasty today, I kept stressing about you all being out there."

"I just had to clear ice from the pond. Sorry I worried you." One of those off-limit feelings he'd doused earlier sparked, burrowing beneath his skin, heating, tenderizing. It was nice to be cared about. Noticed. "The temperature's dropped and it's been snowing like crazy. The roads have to be horrible. I'll give you a ride home in the Jeep."

No way was Gage letting Emma attempt the drive back to Wilder Ranch in her snack-sized car. And it had nothing to do with her driving ability and everything to do with the amount of snow. And the idea of her being out on the roads by herself and something going wrong. Not being able to get ahold of her. Or know if she was okay.

Gage wasn't good with any of the above.

"Ya-ya-ya-ya-ya-ya." A sling of consonants came from Hudson, and then he lunged for Gage.

He gathered the baby against his chest. "Thank you for the agreement, Hudson. I'm glad you've got my back." The baby explored his nose and ears, then gave a shudder that made Gage and Emma laugh. "Are you saying I'm cold, little man?"

Emma sank to a sitting position on the edge of the bed. "But if you drive me then Hudson has to go, too. What if we have trouble or get stuck? Maybe I could just borrow your Jeep and come back in the morning?"

Huh. Gage hadn't thought about the fact that Hudson would have to ride along. Really, neither of them should be driving at this point. But what else were they supposed to do?

A swell of music snaked down the hallway. His phone. Gage must have left it in his coat pocket. He hurried to catch it, carrying Hudson. The boy giggled at the bouncy ride.

Luc's name filled the screen. Surprisingly, Gage managed to answer before it went to voice mail.

"Hey, man. Is my sister still there?"

"Yep, hang on." Emma had followed Gage down the hall, and he offered her the phone. "It's your brother."

Emma took it. "Luc? What's up?"

"I called your phone three times and you didn't answer."

Gage winced. He wasn't trying to eavesdrop, but he could hear everything Luc was saying clear as could be.

"Sorry. Changing a diaper. What's going on? Everyone okay?"

Gage was about to walk away, give them space, but Emma's questions and concern pinned him to the spot.

"We're all good," Luc's voice came through, "but the roads aren't. There's so much snow the plows can't keep up. And some places are icy, too. There's no way you're getting back here tonight."

Gage's saliva turned to dust and his attempt to swallow stuttered and failed.

"I was hoping to catch you before you did something crazy and tried to drive home in that little buggy car of yours."

Emma rolled her eyes at Luc's comment, head shaking. "Gage was planning to drive me home in the Jeep."

She conveniently left out the part about her wanting to take it and go without him.

"Can you put Gage on, too?"

Emma switched the phone to speaker. "Okay, we can both hear you now."

And have been able to this whole time.

"It's an absolute mess out there. Kohl has been rescuing people out of the ditch." Luc's voice jumped down an octave. "Which, strangely enough, he does for fun. He's fished out three cars in the last hour. Gage, do not let Emma leave your house in this. Make her stay."

Make her stay. Pretty much the opposite of his be-careful-around-Emma/don't-let-her-know-how-you're-feeling/protect-her-at-all-costs plan.

But then, sending her out into weather like this, with or without him, wasn't exactly keeping her safe, was it?

Gage forced his voice into functioning mode. "Of course she'll stay. I've got the guest room." Or he could sleep on the couch. "My sister left a few things last time she was here. We'll hunker down."

"Do I get to have an opinion about this?" Emma piped up.

"No," they answered simultaneously.

"Sounds a little like last weekend." She raised an eyebrow at Gage and crossed her arms. But her mouth twitched, which gave him hope that she was teasing.

"What do you want us to say, Em?" Their gazes tangled. Hopefully, his held the softness and caring he felt. "Risking the drive isn't worth it."

Her lips stretched from crescent moon into a full arch. "I agree. I'm just messing with you." She pointed at the phone even though Luc couldn't see her. "But someone has to keep you two meddlers in check."

Luc's low laughter rumbled through the line. "Can't help watching out for you, Emma. You're my baby sister."

Then what was Gage's excuse? Because he definitely did not think of Emma as anything close to a sister.

"And if Mackenzie was out and about, you'd make this same phone call to her?"

"Yes, I'd boss her around, too. Though there's less of a chance of her actually listening."

Emma laughed. "All right, you win. Gage loses because he's stuck with me."

"Ha." Gage's voice came out gravelly and a bit desperate. "Not true." It wasn't that he didn't want Emma around—it was that he did. Exactly why he wished she could make it home tonight. "I'll keep her safe." He barely resisted shaking his head after the words because they sounded chauvinistic. No doubt Emma could take care of herself. But, much like Luc, Gage couldn't resist the urge to protect her.

Even if it was from himself.

"Pretty sure my tab is close to two million now." A freshly showered Gage, dressed in jeans and a long-sleeved Copper Mountain T-shirt peeked over her shoulder at the simmering pasta sauce that Emma stirred. He smelled amazing. Fresh-from-the-shower looked good on him, the tips of his almost black hair shiny from the remaining moisture.

"Methinks you overestimate my value, Counselor."

"And you underestimate." His quirked eyebrow and playful grin ignited those pesky girlish hopes and dreams she'd attempted to dodge over the last few weeks. But they hung on to her like flies on cattle. Not ready to pack up and head out anytime soon.

Gage got out plates from the cupboard for the two of them, then a plastic bowl for Hudson that suction cupped to his high chair tray.

"I don't know how I'm ever going to truly thank you for everything you've done for Hudson and me."

"You just did."

He added silverware to his stack and delivered the items to the table. "You're way too easy on me, Emma. On everyone."

"Oh, stop." Some people made it easy to be easy. She used the wooden spoon to dig a square of ravioli from the boiling water, then tested the softness to see if it was done. Perfect.

Emma placed the stainless steel colander in the sink and dumped the water and pasta in, the steam rising to her face like a mini spa treatment. She closed her eyes and imagined she was in the Wilder hot spring, muscles unwinding, a good book in her hands. Not stuck with Gage and Hudson, even if that's exactly where she wanted—and shouldn't want—to be.

"My new goal is to get you to learn to take a compliment." Gage's voice came from *very* close by, and her eyes popped open to find him at the edge of the sink. He faced her, hip resting against the countertop. "Let's start now. Dinner smells amazing, Emma."

"It's just a jar of marinara sauce and a frozen package of—"

His eyebrows shot to his hairline.

Um. "Thank you?"

He let loose with a deep laugh, the kind that filled the kitchen and had his head jutting back. He grabbed her hand and spun her in a circular dance move as Hudson joined in with a giggle from his play saucer in the living room, banging his sippy cup against the tray.

"Much better." Gage dipped his head until their heights matched, his blue eyes doing that crinkly thing again, rendering Emma a willing victim. "Just don't make it a question next time."

He moved to the stove. "Sauce ready?"

Emma would answer him, but the man had completely messed with her voice box when he'd twirled her around as if them dancing in the kitchen was a normal, everyday occurrence. And suddenly Emma wanted exactly that—on repeat for the next handful of decades.

What was a casual gesture to Gage had taken her out like an amateur on a black diamond slope.

"Emma?"

"Sure." Her answer came out as a croak. "It's ready. We can just add the pasta to the sauce."

He delivered the pot of sauce over to her at the sink and she added the ravioli. Gage moved their dinner to the table while Emma washed her hands with cold water. Not so much because anything was on them, but because she needed a moment to collect herself.

He's not up for grabs. At least not for you. Don't do this to yourself, Emma Wilder. Do not fall for the wrong guy. Again.

"All set?" Gage stood next to the high chair where he'd strapped in Hudson.

Water still cascaded over Emma's now frigid hands. "Yep." She flipped the faucet off and used the towel, then joined them.

Emma cooled ravioli on her plate, cutting it into quarters before scooping it into Hudson's bowl. He dug in, capturing a fistful and attempting to shove the contents into his mouth. Some slipped into the pocket on his bib and he returned for more, slurping in the next batch.

Gage paused with a forkful of salad hovering over his plate. "I think he likes it, and he's not even—" his comment was interrupted by Hudson running a hand through his hair, almost as though he was making sure to cover each individual follicle with red sauce "—making a mess." He finished the statement with slow sarcasm, and they laughed.

Hudson made a silly face, added an overzealous smile, then joined in.

While they ate Gage told her about growing up Frasier. How he and his sister had always been close and that when Nicole had taken off, his sister had flown out to spend a week commiserating with him. Helping him piece his life back together.

Their relationship only reiterated why Gage wanted that same kind of childhood for Hudson. Which was probably a good reminder for Emma. Though she'd never comprehend why Gage didn't realize that he could be that family for the boy, even if it was just him. All it took was love, and Gage had that going for him in spades.

Hudson announced—loudly—that he was done with dinner, so Emma cleaned him up and set him free before he began playing with the food or, worse yet, dropping chunks to the floor as he was apt to do when eating no longer held his attention.

She plunked him down near his toy box, which was a plastic bin stationed at the back of the living room space. Close enough that they could watch his antics. He pulled out an item, chewed on it, then tossed it to the side as Emma rejoined Gage.

When they finished eating, Gage stacked their plates. "I'll do the dishes. You go relax."

What? "No, I'll help." She stood and picked up the ravioli pot. "You've been out in the freezing weather all day. You should be the one crashing."

Gage's hand snaked out and stalled hers, which, in Emma's book, practically qualified as hand-holding. And that showed exactly how few relationships she'd had. Gage peeled her fingers away and took control of the pot. "Not happening." The growl to his voice made her stomach do jumping jacks. "Get out of the kitchen." He flashed a *don't mess with me* grin.

Why did he insist on flirting with her? Did he somehow not understand that doing the dishes equaled exactly that?

Her arms crossed of their own accord, the toe of her boot tapping against the wood floor. "And what do you propose I do with myself while you clean up?"

Propose. Maybe not her best word choice. Not with her standing and Gage sitting. Her mind generated all sorts of farfetched scenarios with that prompt.

"Go read a book. I've no doubt there's one tucked into your purse for emergencies like this."

She laughed. How did he know her that well? "Fine." Emma would argue more, but getting out of the kitchen when Gage was in it might not be a bad idea.

She retrieved the romantic comedy she was currently reading from her purse, left her boots by the front door—she'd put them on earlier when there'd still been a hope of getting home tonight—and dropped onto the couch. Emma covered her lap and legs with a blanket and read with only half of her typical attention span as Gage cleared the table, packed up leftovers, wiped everything down and loaded the dishwasher. Because she had the sinking feeling that any romance going on at the Frasier Ranch was in her heart instead of her book.

Chapter Ten

Hudson emptied his toy bin, tipped it onto its side and crawled into it. He backed out, surveyed his work, then scooted back in, pleased with the game he'd invented. Gage hung the dishcloth to dry on the edge of the sink and joined them in the living room. He lay on the floor by Hudson, and the baby crawled over to him, investigating his long-sleeved shirt and jeans, checking the width of his shoulders, earning a bark, meow, growl or other silly sound when Hudson tugged on his ear, squeezed his nose, or pressed a finger into his cheek. This was obviously not their first go-around with this game, and Emma suddenly felt every inch the intruder. The stalker. And yet, she stayed glued to the spot. She was finally getting a glimpse of Gage and Hudson's evening ritual, and it was enough to make her consider an all-out toddler tantrum.

Because she wanted all of *this*. She was never going to get it with Gage, but she kept leaning in his direction anyway. Not heeding all of the warning signs directing her to turn around. Head the other direction. Anywhere but here.

God, isn't it a waste for a guy like that not to get married and have a family someday? I'm not even saying he has to be for me...though that would be nice if You're taking impossible requests. Can't You change his mind?

No reply resounded in her soul. No affirmative whisper that she'd be awarded the answer to her prayers. If only God would grant her some understanding. Because watching Gage be so amazing with Hudson while knowing he didn't believe he was the right fit to be the baby's guardian hurt her in soul-deep places.

Unable to resist their pull, Emma closed her book and deposited it on the coffee table, then joined Gage and Hudson on the floor. Gage sat up and offered her a toe-tingling grin. A welcome that settled into her bones, cementing her to the spot.

"Where did this come from, by the way?" Emma spun a dial on a new toy that had appeared yesterday. It was full of gadgets for Hudson to explore. Some that squeaked and others that spun. "Did you go pick up more of Hudson's things?"

"No, I...ordered it." Gage scooted the base up, turning it into a walker. "I saw it and thought it would be perfect for when he's ready to start walking. He's been trying to stand more, lately, and I wasn't sure how fast it would all go." He shrugged, endearing. "I like to be prepared."

But what if you give him away before then? Emma didn't crush any of Gage's sweet spirit, but her own was drowning.

"It's perfect for him. He'll love it. Already does."

By the time Hudson's bedtime approached, the ups and downs of watching Gage interact with Hudson had left Emma feeling as if she'd run the emotional gamut of a 5K.

"I'll read to him a little before bed." Gage picked up Hudson, switching to the recliner. A basket of books was stationed to one side.

Gage read about rubber ducks while Emma meandered into the kitchen. Her phone was on the butcher-block island, and she checked it. A new email had come in from a girl who would be helping in Kids' Club this summer. She wanted to know if her boyfriend could apply for a job, too. Emma's nose wrinkled. Wilder Ranch didn't have a hard and fast rule about staffers not dating, but something about this scenario smelled like trouble. Especially with them coming in already attached. She told the girl to have her boyfriend contact Mackenzie about a wrangler position. And then Emma sent a quick text to her sister outlining her concerns over the situation.

Kenzie would handle it from there.

"And the tractor goes vroom."

Gage's deep voice reading to Hudson curled inside of Emma. Warm. Liquid.

"The cow goes moo."

And the girl goes swoon. How was Emma supposed to resist Gage reading to Hudson? That was like the mother ship calling her home.

When he paused to switch books, Emma turned. "Should I make him a bottle?"

Crinkly eyes flashed with gratitude as Hudson gummed the corner of their next book. "That would be great. Thanks."

Emma put the ingredients together and shook the bottle. She met Gage and Hudson at the butcher-block island. "Want me to put him down?"

"That's okay. I've got him." Hudson lunged for the bottle and then crashed back into Gage's arms.

"Good night, sweet boy." Emma kissed his forehead, ran a hand over his incredibly soft hair. "Sleep well."

"You pick out a movie for us to watch while I lay him down. And make it a chick flick. Those are my favorite." Gage winked and took off down the hall.

Silly man. As if Emma would force him to watch one of her movies.

Though, if they were going to watch a movie of any sort, popcorn was a necessity. Emma crossed to the cupboards, found the oil and a pot. She'd become quite at home in Gage's kitchen since Hudson's arrival.

By the time Gage came back, the kernels were sizzling. The newness of the situation—of it being just them— slithered along her spine. Awareness danced through her.

"Thought I'd make some popcorn." The *ting-ting* of popcorn hitting the lid filled the kitchen.

Duh. He could probably have figured that one out on his own. No more needless explanations or filling the silence. Chill already. You can be alone with the guy and be normal. Or at least pretend not to be shaking in your boots about it.

"Sounds good. What can I do to help?"

"Melted butter would be great."

Gage got out a small dish and lopped off some butter, then microwaved it.

"Hey, just so you know, we have a group this next weekend. It's only one day—Saturday. There's no Kids' Club, but we're all going to pitch in and help so that we don't have to hire temps." During the summer they had staff that stayed at the ranch, but this time of year, it was better to hire on an as-needed basis. And for a group this size that was only using the lodge space for the day, it was better to handle it themselves and save the money. "So I'll be here Saturday morning for a few hours to watch Hudson and then I'll plan to head home around noon."

"Okay, no problem." Gage opened the microwave and removed the now-liquid butter. "Glad you let me know. And good job not thinking we can't live without you over here. I mean, we can't, but we'll still be fine."

Sweet man. Emma laughed. "I'm only a phone call away if something is wrong."

"And that's exactly why I'm not going to panic."

She mixed the popcorn in a large bowl, adding butter, salt, and then they moved into the living room.

Panic of the thirteen-year-old girl variety at being trapped in the vicinity of a boy ignited. How should they sit? Should she have poured some into a second dish so that Gage could occupy the recliner?

Emma's steps stuttered when she reached the middle of the couch. "Should I get another bowl?"

Gage's head tilted, questioning. "No need. Let's just sit on the couch."

Right. Which she was completely and totally fine with. Heart palpitations could be a good thing, right? Certainly Emma could find an internet doctor to confirm her self-diagnosis.

She dropped onto the far cushion. Gage did the same on the other side of the sofa. And she placed the popcorn between them.

A buffer. Just in case she got any crazy ideas about putting the moves on Gage during the movie. And by that she meant holding hands. Letting her head rest on his shoulder.

Gage tossed her the remote. "Okay, chick flick it up."

"Um, no."

"Why not? I have zero doubt that you'd choose that if I wasn't here."

"True."

"So hit me with it."

"Are you trying to punish yourself?"

"I'm just extending my apology from last weekend."

"Oh, stop. What would you watch if I wasn't here?"

Gage fisted some popcorn. "Not sure. Maybe SportsCenter. Or a documentary. But that will just put me to sleep tonight. So you're up, batter. Swing."

The remote burned into her palm—a hot potato. "You are awfully bossy tonight, Gage Frasier."

"And you, Emma Wilder, need to stop overthinking and worrying about what I would want to watch. No people pleasing. Just pick something that you like."

"Fine."

Gage's answering chuckle was warm and low and sweet as chocolate. Not helping her spastic cardiac issues in the least. Emma clicked through the menu until she found an old favorite. One Gage might possibly enjoy, too.

For the first fifteen minutes of the movie, Gage made a comment here and there—teasing her mostly. And then? Silence. Emma stole a covert glance in his direction. The man's head sagged back against the couch cushion. Out cold. Poor guy had worked himself to exhaustion today. And then her chick flick had coaxed him to sleep like a lullaby.

Or maybe he'd known that he would conk out either way and had wanted her to watch something she would enjoy. That sounded like her Gage.

Her Gage.

There she went again, putting him in boxes he'd never agreed to crawl into.

Emma moved the popcorn bowl to the coffee table, then added a pillow between them as a new shield. She wasn't even sure why. It wasn't like Gage was even remotely leaning her direction. It was just…a reminder to herself that Gage wasn't right for her. That he was off-limits. A no-go. Because the man really didn't want babies someday. And she really did.

In the middle of the movie, Emma got up and used the bathroom. She found the pajamas Gage's sister had left at his house set out for her along with a new toothbrush. She changed and brushed her teeth, then tossed her clothes into the washing machine on a short cycle for tomorrow.

When she returned, she fought the urge to move the pillow barrier she'd established and scoot next to Gage. Nestle in. She could just imagine him waking up with her snuggled against his arm, his confusion evident. Gage patiently explaining that he didn't see her as anything more than Luc's little sister. Probably writing up a contract for her so that she wouldn't mess up those important details again.

The movie finished, and Emma clicked off the television. She managed to maneuver Gage's head to the sofa, propping a pillow underneath it. She hefted the dead weight of his legs up to the cushions and spread a blanket over him. He reminded her of a little boy with those long eyelashes shadowing his cheeks, any stress from the day smoothed from his skin.

Emma turned down the kitchen lights, leaving only the microwave one on, then locked the dead bolt on the front door. After moving her clothes over to the dryer, she eased quietly into Hudson's room and burrowed under the covers on the guest bed.

It should have taken her hours to fall asleep because of the many thoughts tumbling through her mind. Instead, it was only a matter of minutes because she allowed herself a little game of make-believe.

She pretended that this was her life. That Gage was her husband and Hudson her son.

A little imagination couldn't hurt.

Except it did.

Gage woke at Hudson's cry, surprised to find he'd been sleeping on the couch. The last thing he remembered was the opening to the movie. He must have dozed off, abandoning Emma and officially earning the title of Worst Host Ever.

A blanket covered him, and a pillow was wedged between his head and the armrest.

The work of Emma, of course. Best Caregiver Ever.

Hudson wailed again, but it came from the kitchen, not from down the hall. Gage sat up. Emma was next to the sink mixing a bottle, Hudson in her arms.

"Hey."

She glanced over her shoulder and winced. "I was trying not to wake you. Figured you could use the sleep."

Gage joined her in the kitchen, rubbing the tiredness from his eyes. "I didn't even hear him until just now. Sorry."

"You were out cold." Emma finished shaking the bottle, then cradled Hudson. He cupped the middle-of-the-night snack with greedy hands. "Go to bed, Gage. I've got him. You're exhausted. Let me do this."

His eyes prickled with a strange sensation. The woman

was selfless. Emma watched out for him in a way that he wasn't sure he'd ever experienced before outside of his family. She made him want…a future. A wife. A family. Her.

All things that he wasn't sure he had enough faith to try again.

Frustration bubbled up. Why had Emma come into his life now? When it was too late? Gage was already jaded. Used.

"I can feed him." She should be sleeping. The baby wasn't her responsibility, even though she'd come into their lives and cared for him like he was her own. "You should—"

"Nope." Emma swung Hudson in the other direction so that he was protected from Gage's offer, a playful grin sneaking over her shoulder. How was she so awake, so happy even in the middle of the night? "You're not going to win this one, Counselor."

What Gage really wanted to do was wrap his arms around the two of them. Thank Emma for being…her. Press a kiss to her hair, her forehead…and then travel to other distracting destinations like those lips that could hold his attention for hours. Instead, he barely resisted a growl. What was wrong with him? He had to get away from this woman and the way she made him *feel*. Gage had worked hard to shut down after Nicole. To not let all of that disappointment, hurt…even guilt rise to the surface.

And Emma was churning it all up. That and more.

"Fine. Thank you." His words were wooden. Not soft or warm or anything else they should be. Surprise registered in the dash that formed between Emma's eyebrows. In the faint downward turn of her mouth.

Gage didn't stay to explain. Didn't attempt to ease a smile back onto her face. He had to escape before he did something rash. He crashed into his bed and then added an extra pillow, trying to get comfortable. To find a spot that would allow him the peace of sleep instead of replaying how he'd just acted with Emma.

All to avoid kissing her.

No matter how many times Gage warned himself to keep his distance from Emma—that their futures didn't align—the woman kept shining so much light into his world that she blinded him to his past and the mistakes he'd made.

Almost as if her faith could be enough for the two of them. Emma was sunshine and roses and silver linings. She believed wholeheartedly in love. That it could conquer all. And Gage wasn't sure he did anymore.

For him, not having children was a stopgap. A way to ensure that if he ever did marry again and botched things up as badly as he and Nicole had the first time around, at least he wouldn't be taking any innocent little souls down with him. And no one deserved kids more than generous, caring Emma. She was born to be a mom. It was just *in* her. She couldn't stop that desire if she tried, and Gage would never want her to. He couldn't imagine her not having babies.

It would be like Picasso not picking up a paintbrush.

Which was why he *had* to stop thinking of her as he'd begun to: his saving grace, his new beginning, his first thought in the morning and his last at night.

Because she was none of those things for him. Not if he truly cared about her. Not if he wanted her to have the future she deserved.

Chapter Eleven

Emma woke to the sound of Hudson cooing and talking in his portable crib. She pushed out from under the covers and peeked at him. He grinned, a bit of drool pooling in the corner of his mouth.

"Good morning, cutest baby in the universe." She scooped him up and, after a squeeze, laid him on the bed and changed his diaper. She slipped his footed pajama back on, then picked him up and inched the bedroom door open.

Was Gage up? And what kind of mood was he in?

Last night their encounter in the kitchen had been so strange. One minute he'd been himself, and the next he'd boarded up like an abandoned miner's shack in the mountains.

Had it just been tiredness? Or something else?

A note on the floor placed on top of a sweatshirt and some other clothes caught her attention.

Here's some clothes if you need anything. Breakfast is on the stove. Sorry about last night. —G

Whatever had been going on with Gage, Emma

trusted that he had a good reason for it. Her curious self would just like to know what it was.

In the kitchen, she and Hudson found eggs in the frying pan covered with foil. A yellow Post-it note clung to the face of the coffeepot, its message scrawled in permanent marker. *Drink me. Use the caramel creamer I got you in the fridge. You'll thank me later.*

She laughed, and answering happiness crested Hudson's face. "Sweet boy." She pressed kisses to his cheeks, his hair. "What am I going to do with the two of you? Huh? You're both adorable."

Emma made toast to go with the eggs. She and Hudson ate together as he chattered away about nothing and everything. The table was stationed near the sliding glass doors that led out back. Bridal-white snow covered the land. Crisp. New. As if a snow globe had been shaken and then settled.

Maybe Emma would bundle Hudson up and take him outside for a bit if it wasn't too cold. Pull him around on a sled. But then, Gage wouldn't have any snow toys, would he? Emma was used to Wilder Ranch and the supplies they had for winter groups.

When they finished eating, Emma cleaned Hudson up and settled him on the floor in the kitchen. He opened his favorite cupboard that she'd asked Gage not to baby-proof—one filled with Tupperware—and began pulling pieces out, banging on them, tasting.

She chose a white mug from the cupboard, craving a cup of tea. And the man who'd left her notes. Emma got out the variety box of teas as the coffeepot taunted her. Beckoning.

She *could* try it. It had been years since she'd tasted coffee. Maybe her preferences had evolved over time.

She touched the note Gage had left for her, a smile playing on her lips. The coffee Emma could probably live without, but the man who'd made it was tempting her at every turn. She poured a half cup of brown liquid into her mug, then added a generous dollop of creamer. If she was going to taste the stuff, it had better be well covered.

Her first sip was…interesting. A bit too sweet, so she'd gone overboard with the creamer. But not entirely awful. She added another half inch of coffee, stirred, then tried it again. When Mackenzie made coffee, she drank it with only a little half-and-half. Not Emma's favorite in the least. But this? This could grow on her.

A few hours later, Emma was stirring a batch of simmering chili when Gage opened the front door and came inside.

"Hey. How's it going in here?" A gentle note accompanied his greeting, as if he wasn't sure what kind of response to expect from her after last night's hiccup. But Gage didn't need to worry. Emma wasn't the kind to be scared off by a bump. Especially not when she knew that Gage's soul was good to the last drop.

"Great." She set down the spoon on the holder next to the large pot and leaned against the counter, facing him. "How's it going out there?"

"Cold." Gage's pink kissed-by-the-wind cheeks backed up his declaration. He took off his hat and scrubbed a hand through his hair, leaving the ends scattered. Attractive.

"How are the roads?"

"Still not great." He took off his boots, stowed them on the drying mat. "Ford was the only one who made it back this morning. But the sun's peeking through now, so that's good. Should be able to drive you home in a bit." He hung up his coat.

"If things clear up, I can take my car."

Gage crossed over to her, concern wrinkling his brow. "That thing still won't make it out of here."

"Sure it will."

"Emma, it's currently buried in snow. You going to dig your way home?" He paused inches from her, completely distracting her with the rusty, scratchy sound of his voice. "The Jeep can get through way more than your little buggy. I will fight you about this. If you don't let me drive you, you're going to be stuck here another night."

Throw in a ring, a few repeated lines in front of Pastor Higgin and Gage changing his mind about kids, and Emma would pack her suitcases and roll across the threshold of his house right now. "Fine. A ride is great!" She was as fake as a spoonful of Spam.

Gage didn't seem to notice, instead focusing on the browned beef, garlic, onion and spices wafting from the pot on the stove. "What are you making? It smells amazing. My mom must have made something similar when I was growing up, because it brought me right back to childhood."

"It's just chili."

"Just?" His head shook. "What did we discuss last night?"

What was with this man and his compliments? "That you're going to stop making a big deal about everything I do?"

His chuckle warmed her like hot fudge melting ice cream. He was still standing awfully close. He smelled of snow and moisture and Gage and goodness all rolled into one.

"You weren't joking when you said you'd stockpiled groceries."

Her teeth pressed into the corner of her lip. "I'm sorry. I promise I'm not spending too much. And I'd happily pay for it myself if you'd let—"

Gage cut her off by placing his glacial hand over her mouth. "Enough. I'm happy to have food in the house, Em. I could care less about the grocery bill. Do you have any idea how nice it is to come in from out there—" he nodded out back "—and find this? Money can't buy that kind of goodness."

Emma had only computed half of his words because his hand was glued to her lips. She was torn between hoping he'd stay put and rescuing herself from his icy palm. She opted for door number two—the hand removal. "You're freezing! You'd better warm yourself up or you're going to lose a finger to frostbite."

Playfulness sparked in Gage's eyes. "And how do you advise I do that? You offering to help?"

"No." Her answer was quick. Short. And a lie if there ever was one.

"That doesn't seem very sacrificial of you. Are you sure you don't want to reconsider?" He closed the gap between them, hands snaking to rest at the nape of her neck, burrowing under her ponytail.

They were practically in an embrace, his wrists resting on her shoulders, his face so close to hers.

Emma took an exaggerated step back—rather proud of herself for moving away from Gage's touch—and his arms dropped to his sides. "You could run your hands under some hot water. Take a shower. Hold a cup of that coffee you love so much."

His mouth hitched. "But what fun would that be when you're right here in front of me?" Gage lunged for her, and Emma shrieked and took off around the island. She was half laughing, half squealing when Gage caught up to her on the other side of the butcher block. He snagged one wrist, spinning her in his direction before capturing the other. She was trapped. Held captive.

And she suddenly couldn't recall why she was running at all.

What had gotten into him? Last night Gage had been racked with all of the reasons he should tread carefully around Emma. Keep things strictly platonic. And then he'd come inside to find her wearing his sweatshirt—the one he'd set out for her—and his brain had hailed a cab.

Emma's hair was up in a ponytail. She wore jeans and—he glanced down—his slippers. How had she made it around the island in them without falling flat on her face? They must be two sizes too big for her.

She was adorable. Irresistible, it seemed, based on his current actions and the fact that he'd yet to let go of her.

Gage could use a buffer between them. A strong wall. Or a small, squirmy baby. "Where's Hudson?"

"Down for his nap."

So much for that barrier. Emma's eyes still danced and sparkled, and Gage fell right into them. He slid chilly fingers inside the sleeves of the sweatshirt. Goose bumps erupted along the sensitive skin on the inside of her wrists. From the cold? Or from his touch?

"You're going to turn me into a block of ice." If Emma wanted to escape, she could. His hold on her was light, gentle. But she didn't attempt to break free. Her slate-blue eyes held mirth, laughter stifled in the press of her lips.

"I just need you to melt me back to life." The truth hit Gage like running fifty miles per hour smack into a brick wall. That's exactly what Emma had done over the past few weeks. She'd taught him to breathe again. To wake up expectant in the morning. To *live*.

Their gazes met and held, and a rubber band twisted around Gage's lungs, squeezing. Ho-boy. When the playful moment between them had sprouted, Gage hadn't imagined ending up here. Close enough to Emma that he could lean in, taste those scrumptious lips.

His grip slacked, loosened. And then Emma did the strangest thing… She captured his hands and brought them up to her face level, then blew warm air across his now-tingling nerves.

"Better?"

Painfully so. Only Emma would take a situation when he was teasing her and actually attempt to add to his comfort.

Gage gave a nod since he couldn't manage to speak. If he had answered out loud, no doubt his voice would have cracked any syllable into two. His senses screamed and shot into the red zone. He should never have chased Emma. Should have stuck to his plan.

Gage dug deep for a shred of remorse. Anything to stop him from doing what he currently wanted to do.

"I'm sorry I was grumpy and short with you last night."

"Okay." Emma smiled, grace evident, and then repeated her actions, the heat tingling against his skin. "Why were you?"

Her eyes were soft. Tender. Everything he wanted to see was written in them, and despite knowing better, Gage felt himself falling. "Because I was trying not to do this." His head swooped low and his lips found hers as if they'd never had another destination.

Despite all of his self-admonitions over the last few weeks—the reminders of who he was, his mistakes— Gage couldn't resist Emma. Ever since he'd seen her for who she truly was, he'd been heading for exactly this. No chance of turning back.

Emma pressed up on her toes to meet his kiss, sliding her fingers into his hair. Killing him slowly.

Her kiss was a mixture of steady and strong with a hint of abandon wrapped in. She tasted like home. Comfort. Like this was where he was always supposed to be, and he'd missed the directions before and ended up lost.

But kissing Emma made everything right in the world.

It was as if everything up until this point in Gage's life—accomplishment or failure—faded.

He rested his forehead against hers and waited for his skittish pulse to slow.

Waited for her to say something, because he didn't have words.

I'm sorry?

Would you mind if I did that one more time?

Except one more kiss would never be enough. Not when it came to sweet Emma.

"We shouldn't be doing this." He broke the silence.

All of the unspoken reasons wedged between them. A hint of pain pierced her features, plunging a knife through his skin. This wasn't a smart choice for either of them. And hurting her wasn't supposed to be an option.

"Well." Emma's voice came out raspy, and Gage was pathetically pleased the kiss had affected her like it had him. "If we already started...and today is ruined...we might as well go ahead and finish."

His mouth twitched. Curved. "You sound like a lawyer." A cute one. With a very excellent point.

"That's you, Counselor. I'm just stating the facts."

His chest rumbled with laughter. What would one more kiss hurt? Because, as Emma had pointed out, he'd already crashed down a slippery slope and wasn't going to be able to scramble back up without rescue.

"Who am I to argue with such a well-played defense?" Gage ran a thumb over her plump, tempting bottom lip. And then he kissed her again. She made a little sound of contentment. Scooted closer. Cinched the rope she'd already lassoed around him.

A sharp cry came from down the hallway. Emma eased back, eyes crinkling with honeyed remorse. "Time's up."

Disappointment choked him. "Maybe he'll go back to sleep?"

She laughed. Bit her lip.

"Stop it, woman."

She switched to a full-fledged, knock-him-over-with-a-feather grin.

Another howl came from Hudson. This one annoyed. As if questioning why someone hadn't come to free him yet. Then a string of demanding babbles followed.

They both laughed.

Hudson was not to be deterred. Probably a good thing considering what Gage and Emma had just been doing. "I'll get him." Gage took off down the hall. He should be thankful for Hudson's interruption. The chance to rein himself in. Head back to the land of logic. Of knowing that he should never have kissed Emma. But mostly, he was enduring the crushing blow of awareness that what had just transpired between them could never happen again.

Chapter Twelve

"Aunt Emma," Ruby piped up from the back seat as Luc gave Emma a ride back to Gage's the next morning, "will baby Hudson be awake when we get there?"

"He should be, honey." This morning Cate had been up early with nausea, so Luc had brought Ruby with them in order to give her some space.

"Yay!" Ruby clapped with excitement. "I'm going to teach him the ABC's and we're going to count to ten and then we'll have recess. And I'll tell Ms. Robin tomorrow that I practiced school today." Ruby's preschool had canceled this morning because so many people traveled into town for it and some of the rural roads still weren't in great condition. Much to the girl's displeasure.

"Sounds perfect, Rubes. Hudson can't really talk yet. He pretty much makes noises and sounds. But whatever you do, he'll love."

Luc turned down Gage's drive, and the sun reflected off of the unspoiled, sparkling snow, practically blinding them. He parked, and the three of them got out of the truck. Gage held the front door open, Hudson in one arm. Ruby squealed with delight at the sight of the baby and took off at a run. Luc followed.

Emma fell in step behind him.

What would it be like with Gage today after their lip-lock yesterday? Would it be uncomfortable? Or would they just go on as if it hadn't happened?

They hadn't discussed anything after The Kiss that would forever outrank any other kisses. By the time they'd gotten Hudson up from his nap, changed his diaper and fed him, Luc had unexpectedly shown up to offer Emma a ride home.

Her brother—her knight in a shining pickup truck. How utterly unromantic.

Emma understood Gage's reasoning behind putting on the brakes during The Kiss, but overnight, her opti-mism and imagination had birthed a baby. She'd begun wondering if it was possible that Gage might change his mind about his preconceived notions and decide that all he wanted was her.

And Hudson.

She'd never denied being a dreamer.

But despite any niggling fears over Gage's *we shouldn't be doing this* reaction to their kiss, Emma didn't regret it. In fact, she'd gladly participate all over again.

But then, she believed in love with a capital *L*—the conquer-anything kind. Gage, on the other hand, was still blooming back to life. She doubted that he was ready to toss his beliefs about marriage and kids to the wayside and saddle up with her. Even if that's what her dreams had included last night.

They tromped inside. Gage settled Hudson onto the living room floor, and Ruby joined him. She asked him questions he babbled answers to while she pressed every button on every toy that made noise. Hudson was completely enthralled with the girl and the ruckus.

Emma hung her coat in the closet. Took off her lined black ankle rain boots. She'd dressed for comfort today—gray leggings and a black hip-length sweater. She had her hair up in a bun, almost in an effort to prove that she wasn't primping for Gage. Though she had applied makeup—mascara, a touch of lip gloss. A girl had to feel good about herself, especially if the guy she wanted didn't echo the sentiment.

You don't know that for sure. Try for some patience. Who knew what today held? Maybe Emma wasn't crazy to harbor a little hope.

"Coffee?" Gage offered, mostly to Luc, his attention bouncing quickly from her.

What did you expect, girl? You already knew how the game would end when you jumped into the arena.

"Sounds great." Luc followed Gage into the kitchen. "For some reason the smell of coffee is turning Cate's stomach in the morning. I keep running over to the lodge to make it for myself."

Emma stood indecisively between the kitchen and the living room. Where did she belong? With Luc and Gage? Or the baby and Ruby?

And if she joined the guys, would her brother somehow know that she'd been standing just across the island yesterday when Gage had blown her mind with a kiss so tender and yet smoking that she'd momentarily forgotten her own name?

Since Hudson was happily entertained by Ruby, Emma joined her brother and Gage in the kitchen. She picked a red mug from the cupboard and poured herself a small cup of coffee.

After retrieving the creamer from the fridge, she added a dollop. Gage and Luc's conversation about how the cattle were faring in the snow screeched to a dead halt behind her.

Emma turned, palming her drink. Both men stared at her—Luc with complete confusion, Gage with an all-out grin. His gaze landed on the coffee in her hands, then bounced back to her face, and an electrical current surged between them. So that did still exist. It hadn't just been in her imagination. The Kiss played across the big-screen movie theatre in her mind, and, oh, how she wanted to snuggle in with a blanket and some popcorn and hang out for a bit. Experience it all over again.

"I wondered if you'd tried it yesterday," Gage said.

"It's not as bad as I'd remembered." Emma lifted a shoulder, drinking Gage in until she feared that her brother would catch wind of the attraction between them—at least on her side—and confront them right then and there about what was going on.

After his smile kicked into magnetic levels, she tore her eyes away.

"Since when do you drink coffee?" Luc nodded toward the mug cupped between her hands.

"Since yesterday. Gage has been forcing me—"

"Ahem," Gage interrupted.

"*Persuading* me to try it. It might be growing on me." Or maybe that was the man himself.

A few minutes later, when Luc told Ruby it was time to go, she shook her head. "No, not yet, Daddy. We need to stay a couple two more minutes."

Between the sugary lilt of her voice, the Ruby-ism and the *Daddy*, Luc would be toast. "I know you want to stay, Rubes, but Dad has to get some work done."

The girl's lips quivered with earthquake velocity. "But I don't want to go home yet. Hudson and I were playing so nicely together."

Emma managed to stifle the laugh that begged to escape. *Well played, little one.*

"Ruby, you should grow up to be a lawyer." Gage lifted his coffee cup in a salute. "All of the women in your family seem to have a gift when it comes to closing arguments." He raised an eyebrow at Emma, causing her cheeks to heat and flame. Thankfully, her brother faced Ruby, his back to them.

"Luc." Emma touched his arm, her voice low. "I can keep her. I'm sure Gage doesn't mind." Why hadn't Emma thought earlier to have her stay for the day? Ruby would be a help with entertaining Hudson, and it would give Cate a day to rest and grow some beautiful babies. Two birds, one stone.

Though, knowing Cate, the minute she felt even remotely better, the woman would be back at her computer, designing whatever freelance graphic design project was due next.

"Not at all." Gage dumped the last sip of his coffee into the sink and loaded it into the dishwasher along with Luc's. "Totally up to Emma, but I'm good with whatever."

"Are you sure? That's a lot for you to handle."

Emma laughed. "Two kids compared to twenty or more? I think I'll be just fine."

Luc shook his head in wonder. "And pretty soon our household will be up to a total of three of them. Crazy to think." He hugged Emma. "Thanks, sis. You're the best."

"I like to think so." When she preened, Luc half laughed, half groaned. He said goodbye to Ruby—who wasn't the least bit concerned over his departure—then took off.

Gage bundled up to head outside, and Emma busied herself in the kitchen even though there really wasn't anything to do. But she wasn't going to stand by the front door and expect a *bye, honey, have a great day smooch* from Gage.

Sadly.

Instead of heading out the door, Gage rounded the island, then paused in front of her. Emma's breath stuttered in her lungs, stalling. His hair was in a bit of disarray this morning, but that only served to make it more attractive. Muscle memory flared, the feel of it igniting on her fingertips even though her hands were currently nowhere near him.

"Em." His eyes asked questions and demanded answers she didn't plan to give. "About yesterday…"

He'd better not apologize. Or say anything including the word *kiss*. Because while Ruby was currently captivated with Hudson, her little ears could be quite perceptive when they wanted to be.

"I shouldn't have…and I'm—"

"Don't you dare apologize, Gage Frasier." Amazingly, Emma's voice remained low and even while she quickly came to terms with the fact that her fanciful hopes and dreams were exactly that. Gage hadn't changed his mind overnight about everything he believed to be true.

Ouch. The blow cut deeper than she'd expected.

Emma read so much remorse and care on his face. Concern, but not love. Nowhere near that. "We want different things for the future, and I—"

"Stop!" Emma raised a finger. "I don't want to hear it." She considered pressing it against his lips to still any more words from tumbling out, but that kind of touch right now—contact with the place she wanted to experience again and wouldn't—might send her crashing to the floor.

Emma didn't need to hear that their futures didn't align. She already knew. It already hurt. And Gage, being the gentleman he was, would never take advantage of her. Never let a relationship happen when he didn't plan to have children and she did.

Gage's eyes were soft. "Fine. You win. No apologies. But we're good? Because if I'd ruined our friendship, I'd never forgive myself. And I don't want to mess things up for Hudson, either. He needs you."

Emma had never before managed a conversation while being repeatedly stabbed. She let the waters of disappointment cover her head. Tug her under. Maybe she didn't need to surface. Not today.

"We're just fine." Resignation laced the lie. Emma was usually a big proponent of the truth, but in this case, it would only cause harm. So she would allow herself the sin and take the punishment that went with it.

"It's not you, Em. Not in the least. But I don't want—"

Kids. "I understand." She interrupted, unable to hear him say it out loud right now. Knowing that she wasn't enough to change his mind. "But don't apologize. Because I'm not sorry."

Even if Gage had glimpsed for just a few seconds how she felt about him, Emma would consider that a victory. Because someday, somehow, she wanted him to experience love again. The all-encompassing, no-holding-back kind. The kind that he refused to go anywhere near.

Gage framed her face with one hand, thumb tattooing his touch across her cheekbone. "Then I'm not, either."

Unspoken loss echoed between them. His hand crashed to his side. "I'm glad I didn't hurt you."

She hadn't said those words, but if that's what he'd gathered, Emma would let him rest in that mistaken knowledge.

And really, none of this was his fault. Emma had stridden into this wall of pain willingly. She'd seen the attack coming—the turmoil that falling for Gage would cause—and she'd marched right into battle. As she was apt to do. She had a tendency to leap. To believe in people. In mended hearts and good intentions.

Just like she had with James.

And now, here she was, repeating the same mistakes with Gage. Only he wasn't anything like James. Except for the fact that he was all wrong for her.

Gage didn't want her. Not like that. Or at least not enough to even consider changing his mind about marriage. Kids. And still, she'd jumped right in without a life preserver. Without caring what would happen to her when things didn't work out.

Gage walked to the front door, then paused with his hand on the knob. "Hey, will you go to Denver with me tomorrow afternoon? I have to drop off stuff at my old firm, and then we could shop for clothes for Hudson. Didn't you say his things are getting small and that he needs the next size up?"

"I did."

"I'm not sure what to get him, and I thought maybe you could come. But it's okay if you can't."

I can't. Any more time she spent with Gage now would be like skinning the same knee over and over again without time for healing between collisions. The wound digging deeper with each impact.

But what was she going to do? Tell him that? If Emma wanted to keep watching Hudson—which she did—then she had to pretend that all was well. That being with Gage wasn't wonderful and painful all at the same time.

Because if the man discovered her feelings, he would want to protect her. To separate them and somehow spare her this agony.

"Sure." Tears built in the back of her throat, choking, climbing into her eyes. "Sounds great."

And like it might kill me.

Now Emma just had to make sure that Gage didn't find out how far she'd fallen.

Emma held up a onesie with *rock star* scrawled across the front. "Isn't this cute?"

"Sure. It's great," Gage added some enthusiasm to his tone, thinking maybe if he did, Emma would actually pick out items instead of just looking at them. "Put it in the cart."

Her hand landed against her sternum, her dramatic expression exaggerated. He hoped. "When a person shops, they have to really *shop*. Not just browse and toss items into the cart. What fun would that be?"

"The fast kind?"

Raised eyebrows turned Emma into a schoolteacher about to reprimand Gage…or send him to the principal's office. A pretty one. She wore leg-hugging jeans, brown leather ankle boots, and a slate-blue shirt that so perfectly matched her eyes that Gage had been mesmerized by them since she'd arrived at his house earlier this morning.

"Real shopping is comparing different things to make sure it's definitely what you want." Emma's first-grade level explanation only added to the teacher scenario he'd just conjured. She held the onesie against another of the same. Checking sizes or torturing him—he wasn't sure. "It can't be rushed."

Gage wrinkled his nose. "I don't think I like this turn of events."

Mirth danced in her eyes. "Well, this is definitely a yes, so I *will* put it in the cart." A sassy, kissable grin accompanied her statement.

Whoops. There he went again, reliving that moment in his kitchen. Or wishing he could.

"All right, he needs pants. His are getting short." Emma drove the cart with Hudson in it, and Gage followed like a lost puppy. He'd imagined shopping to be walking into a store—one, not the two they'd already been to—and picking out a couple packages of clothes. Done. He hadn't understood exactly what he was bargaining for with Emma in the lead.

Not that he'd know what to buy for Hudson without her.

"What do you think of these?" She held up some miniature khakis that had a zipper by the thigh—a style choice, Gage assumed, since it didn't actually accomplish anything. One that Hudson would probably find distracting and interesting.

"They look good to me."

"I'm not sure this fabric is strong enough at the knees. Especially with him crawling like he is."

"How long will he wear them? How sturdy do they need to be?"

"Good point. He's growing so fast it will probably only be a few months. And he's starting to pull up and cruise a bit." She analyzed the pants with an intensity and time commitment someone might reserve for Olympic training.

Emma was cute when she shopped. Or took a breath. Or flashed a smile at him without knowing that it rendered him as helpless as a newborn calf in a snowstorm.

And even though the woman could turn shopping into a decathlon, he was somehow still enjoying himself.

Being with Emma did that to him, it seemed, no matter where they were. And if Emma could make shopping for baby clothes tolerable, she could literally hold the moon in the sky with her pinky finger.

Though at the rate they were going, she'd have them in another three stores before she found the "right" things for Hudson. And all of this for a ten-month-old baby!

"Can't believe he's already in twelve-month clothes." Emma pressed a kiss to Hudson's forehead. "You are such a big boy." He latched on to a lock of her hair. "Ouch." She froze and tried untangling, but Hudson had homed in quick.

Gage rescued her, unraveling her hair from Hudson's fingers. Emma smelled edible. Was it her shampoo that had the vanilla scent? Or her skin?

At least Gage had plenty of time to analyze his questions while Emma *shopped.*

She switched to a different pair of pants while Hudson threw his teething ring to the ground. Gage picked it up. Wiped it against his plaid button-up shirt. Good enough. The five-second rule counted, right?

When he gave it back to Hudson, the boy just tossed it again. Hudson's code for *all done.* Gage unbuckled the strap holding him hostage. *I feel you, buddy.* The kid had already been distracted by various toys and fed numerous snacks. Cart time had officially come to an end.

Hudson's weight settled against Gage's arm along with a foreign sense of peace. Gage hadn't expected to bond so quickly with the baby. But Emma had been right that love covered a multitude of inadequacies.

It was amazing to think about how much Hudson had changed since his arrival. And crushing to think about how much Zeke had missed. His friend's absence was palpable. Constant and sharp. An image of Zeke ignited. Shaved head, easy grin. Confident. Gage would give just about anything to talk to him and ask for advice on how to best provide for Hudson. Ask if Gage was right to find another two-parent, unjaded family for the boy.

Hudson complained at the lack of movement or entertainment, so Gage began flying him through the various clothing racks. Fussing turned to approval and laughter. Hudson had the best laugh. But then, so did Emma. And the pair of them were turning into his favorite place to be. What was he supposed to do about that?

"Okay, baby, I hear you." Emma ran a hand over Hudson's hair as they zoomed by. Her next comment was for Gage. "I think I'm losing him."

You think?

If she wasn't so adorable, she'd have lost Gage an hour ago. If only there was some sort of reward system for shopping that might make things more…interesting. Like, if he knew the evening would end with a repeat of that kiss from the other day… Well, then he might just be willing to fit in another five stores.

His lips twitched at the thought.

He paused next to Emma during a flyby. "If you wrap this up in the next few minutes—" *like Hudson and I are hoping* "—I'll take you to dinner. Anywhere you want."

He sent Emma his most pleading look, and Hudson, the little ham, duplicated his facial expression.

Emma's eyes softened with unsung amusement. "Stop it, you two."

"A steak dinner?" Even though Gage had plenty of steaks in his freezer at home, he'd gladly pay if it would convert Emma's browsing into purchases.

Emma's nose wrinkled, her mouth wobbling as she battled a smile. "Bribery only works on children."

Not true. "Some kind of fancy pasta?" A faint amount of interest was piqued. "Indian food?" No give. "Mexican?" What was he not thinking of?

"I'm really more of a burger, fries and a milkshake, girl, Counselor. You're barking up the wrong tree."

Leave it to Emma to want something simple. Not expensive.

"I know the perfect place. Local beef, hand-cut fresh potato fries." Intrigue flashed. He had her now. "And they make malts that are to die for." He added a dramatic flair to his closing statements.

Hangers zipped along the metal rack as Emma flipped through clothing items. "Fine." A begrudging curve split her cheeks. "I'll make some choices."

Gage whooped and tossed Hudson into the air. He caught him and then spun in a circle, creating a mini-parade around the clothing section. Hudson approved of Gage's antics, and based on the way Emma's mouth curved, she did too.

Hudson's professional shopper settled on a pack of onesies—Gage's original idea, thank you very much—plus four pairs of pants, socks, two pajamas, three additional shirts, one with collar, two without. Gage was smart enough not to comment about how fast Emma had picked things out once a bribe was in place. Ahem.

The three of them headed for the checkout. Gage paid and grabbed the bags while Emma parked the cart and bundled Hudson into his coat and fox-eared hat. They were almost to the exit when Gage heard his name.

He turned. Jonas—a guy whose wife had been friends with Nicole since junior high—headed their way. Gage fought the urge to duck and run. He'd prefer no interaction with anything Nicole had tainted—especially with Emma and Hudson in tow—but he had nothing against Jonas.

They shook hands, exchanged greetings. "It's good to see you, Gage. What's it been? Two-and-a-half years?"

"Sounds about right." And what did Gage have to show for it? Bitterness. Guilt. A determination not to move into the future. To stay…frozen. The thought made his stomach lurch. He hadn't realized what he was doing with holding back from the idea of keeping Hudson—and Emma—in his life. From shoving past his Nicole issues into a future he could look forward to, not just a barren, lonely one.

"This is Hudson and Emma." His…ward? Friend? Neither of those labels did the two of them any justice, so Gage let the words die on his tongue.

Jonas nodded at Emma, amusement surfacing when Hudson babbled in greeting and then shoved fingers into his mouth, creating a *ppfftt* sound.

"Cute kid. So you're really a cowboy, huh, Frasier?"

Gage laughed. "I don't know if I've earned that title quite yet. My uncle's foreman stayed on after he passed, and he taught me what I know. But I do enjoy ranching." That truth surprised him, quickly morphing into certainty. It wasn't just an escape like it had started out being. It was a choice he'd make all over again.

They caught up for a few minutes, and then Jonas glanced at his watch. "I've got to run, but it was nice bumping into you. I'm glad to hear you're doing well." A warm grin included Emma and Hudson. "And that you have a great family. I always thought you deserved that."

A great family. Jonas took off before Gage could correct him. But what was he going to say anyway? They're not mine? Not for keeps? And…what if he wanted them to be?

Ever since Gage and Emma had locked lips, his rational side had been kicked to the curb. What if he'd been wrong all this time and God had something new and scary and amazingly good all rolled together in store for him? Could Gage even allow himself to think like that? He'd believed that he didn't deserve another chance when he and Nicole had botched things up so badly the first time.

But he was starting to want one.

"Ready?" Emma's head quirked to one side, and she studied him with a faint smile. Curious. Patient.

"Yep." His fingers itched to hold her hand, but once they broke out into the cold weather, Emma gave a little yelp and took off jogging.

"I need summer back." Her voice shot over her shoulder.

Gage laughed and ran to catch up with them, digging the key fob from his pocket to unlock the doors. He opened the back and stowed the items while Emma secured Hudson into his car seat.

They made a good team.

Emma climbed into the passenger seat. "Brr!"

Gage shut the back and headed for the driver's door. He opened it to the sound of Emma's bright laughter echoing through the vehicle. "Hudson just tried to imitate my *brr*. It was so funny." She twisted, directing her voice to the back row. "You are the cutest boy in the whole universe, Sir Hudson. It's a tough job, but somebody has to do it."

The boy's car seat faced backward, but he made a silly noise and lifted his arms as if receiving accolades.

Gage's heart slowed. Turned mushy. If he could pause or press the slow-motion button to hoard time, he would. Somehow Emma had no idea that she was the most charming woman in the whole world. And Gage wanted to tell her. To lean over the console and kiss her and not apologize for it afterward.

He wanted things that he hadn't allowed himself to dream about in years, and he didn't know what to do about that. But he was definitely going to mull and pray over these new developments.

What if he'd been wrong about marriage and relationships? Even keeping Hudson? Could he change from the man who'd been married to Nicole—who'd made mistakes and failed miserably—into someone else? And if he did attempt that kind of overhaul, would he be enough?

Because he certainly hadn't been the last time.

Chapter Thirteen

Emma couldn't put her finger on exactly what was different with Gage. But something had shifted last night. Somewhere between shopping, dinner and the drive home—during which she and Hudson had both fallen asleep.

This morning when she'd arrived to watch Hudson for a few hours, Gage had lingered. He'd had an extra cup of coffee. Sat with her at the table while she'd fed Hudson oatmeal. Almost as if he hadn't wanted to leave her presence.

Numerous times Emma had gotten the distinct impression that Gage wanted to tell her something. His mouth would open, then snap shut. His head would shake. But he didn't fill her in. Didn't open up.

Yes, Emma was quite certain something was different.

If only she knew what.

"Whoa." Gage caught Hudson as he cruised along the couch and sniffed his diapered bum. "There is no question about what's in here." He switched to holding him.

"That is impressively disgusting, and I deal with cattle on a daily basis."

Emma laughed as she rounded up toys, tossing them into the bin.

"I'm going to change him and lay him down for his nap, and you should head out."

Gage had come in from working at noon since she had to head home to help with the group at Wilder Ranch.

He gave an exasperated sigh when she kept tidying and then crossed over to her, taking a toy from her hand and tossing it into the bin. "I can handle cleanup duty. Enough."

What's going on with you, Counselor? What are you not telling me?

"I don't have to leave quite yet." A few more minutes wouldn't hurt.

"Oh." That toe-tingling grin of his slid into play. "Good. Then I'll be right back."

She watched his retreating back, mouth curving at the way he talked to Hudson. Like they were old acquaintances. Like being named as Hudson's guardian hadn't held him under water for a good long while.

Emma paused from her task of rounding up Hudson's blocks when a knock sounded at the door.

"Em, can you get that?" Gage's voice boomed from down the hall, and her lips formed a happy little curve at the shortened version of her name. Other people called her the same, but when Gage did, it was somehow… better.

"Sure." Hurrying over to open the door, she was about to explain why it was her answering instead of Gage when the identities of the two people on Gage's front step registered.

Nicole. And James.

That moment in elementary school when Emma's teacher had asked if she was going to be sick and she'd answered no just before her breakfast had covered her teacher's shoes was happening all over again.

What were the two of them doing here? And if she slammed the door in their faces, would they go away?

Nicole was dressed in slimming jeans and leather knee-high boots. Her raven hair fell in loose waves around her striking face. Just her appearance took a spoon to Emma's gut.

She'd forgotten what a bombshell the woman was. Nicole was a perfect, curvy-in-only-the-right-places size two.

And Emma was a medium.

James had aged. He seemed harder around the edges. And the scruffiness that had once appealed now…didn't.

Why had Emma ever dated him? Why hadn't she seen his true colors right away? Emma had never told Gage about having dated James because there hadn't been a reason to. It wasn't like he'd asked her out. Or kissed her again. Or held her hand on the way home last night. Granted, she'd been sleeping, but still. There'd been no blatant sign from him that he was interested in pursuing a relationship with her, and therefore no reason to share her embarrassing past with him.

Plus, Emma hadn't wanted to ruin all of the changes in Gage since Hudson's arrival by bringing up something that would derail him.

Yet now her past had arrived on the front step.

"That might be his best worst diaper yet." Gage's humorous comment as he came down the hall sans Hudson would normally have made her laugh, but any amusement had fled Emma's body when she'd opened the door and recognized his visitors. She wanted to warn him, but what should she say? Run? Take cover?

Before she could scrounge up a solution, Gage was next to her. The air in his lungs spilled out as if he'd fielded a sledgehammer blow. Emma wanted nothing more than to turn into him and wrap her arms around his middle. Shield him, somehow.

If James mentioned anything about dating Emma—though she didn't know why he would—Gage would find out in the worst possible manner. He'd consider it a betrayal that she hadn't told him. Even though it was within her rights not to. He wouldn't understand. Not when he'd been so blinded by Nicole. When he'd endured so much misery by disloyalty.

"I should let you…" She glanced at Gage. He'd schooled his features. Shut down. "I'm just going to go." Emma's purse was in the front closet only a few steps away. Escape was within her reach. She could practically feel the warmth of her jacket. The freedom of her car taking her far, far away from this turmoil.

"No." Gage held her wrist gently as she stepped toward the closet, his thumb finding her pulse. "Please stay. These two are the ones who need to leave."

His appeal was quiet, tender. How could Emma refuse?

Of course James and Nicole didn't move.

Gage had paused Emma's getaway, leaving her right smack-dab in the middle of all of the tension. She scooted next to him, her shoulder touching his arm. Emma found his hand and squeezed. She'd only planned on the short burst of encouragement, but Gage held on like she was his lifeline.

"What do you want, Nicole?" He sounded worn. Frayed. Gage didn't even acknowledge James.

"Can't we come in? It's freezing out here." Nicole's whine turned to puffs of white as it escaped, and she rubbed the sleeves of her North Face jacket, mouth forming a pout.

Ick. The woman could teach classes—Manipulation 101.

No doubt Gage was treading in the same *what was I thinking* waters as Emma had moments before.

"Fine." The word snapped with irritation. Gage stepped back from the open door, keeping Emma with him and leaving only enough space for Nicole and James to move a few feet inside. His stance blocked their entry into the living room, as if intent on barricading them from worming too far into his world. Emma understood the sentiment. She still wouldn't mind a quick escape from The Most Uncomfortable Situation Ever.

Hello, Gage's ex-wife. Pretty sure I'm in love with the man you treated like trash. Does he love me back? No. No, he does not. But these next few minutes should be loads of fun. So glad I'm here for the festivities.

James shut the door as Nicole zeroed in on their joined hands. "Rumor on the street is that you got that precious little family you always wanted."

"Where'd you hear that?"

"April." Narrowed eyes accompanied Nicole's response.

Who? Emma glanced to Gage. "Jonas's wife." Gage answered her silent question, but his wary eyes never left Nicole and, subsequently, James, who so far had stayed quiet. Why was he here? It wasn't as if Nicole needed protection to talk to Gage.

But then, that sounded like exactly the kind of story this woman would weave. No doubt James had come along as a bodyguard. Unless the idea of showing up here was his…

Emma's stomach twisted like a washing machine on spin cycle. She knew firsthand how calculating James could be.

Jonas had called them a family last night, and Gage hadn't corrected him. He'd left too quickly for either of them to contradict him. At the time, Emma had thought it wouldn't matter if he'd mistakenly believed they were together. But she could see now that it did.

But why did the woman care? She and Gage were long over. What was this all about?

"Jonas said the baby was probably around a year old," Nicole continued. "Maybe even older." Close but not quite. "Just how fast did you move on after I left? Or was it before? I'm starting to wonder if you were the one who stepped out on me, and our divorce settlement needs another look."

So she was here for money.

Gage's arm that pressed into Emma's went rigid. "That's what you came here for? More money? I was far too easy on you in the divorce, and you know it."

Before Nicole could speak again, Gage released his hold on Emma, stepped around them and opened the door. "Your accusations and threats are off base, and they're not going to work. Don't ever ask me for more again or I will take legal action."

Was that legit? Legal action? Or was Gage bluffing? Either way, Emma barely resisted a cheer. Or the desire to turn Nicole toward the exit and then give her a very Christian, gentle, prayer-filled nudge.

Nothing too physical. More of a "see you later, don't come back again" exclamation point to Gage's dismissal.

James stepped between Nicole and Gage, and a chill skated along Emma's spine. Something about him was dark. Menacing. "Emma, you should tell your man to rethink his choice."

Cold eyes met hers.

"Get out." Gage's voice ramped up to hurricane velocity. Deep. Twisting. His patience had flown out the open door, it seemed.

Anger radiated from James, and the flash of retribution that sparked constricted Emma's lungs. *No, no, no.* He was going to throw her under the bus like a chewed-up apple core. She *knew* it. Felt it down to the marrow of her bones. "Interesting switch we've got going here, isn't it?" He spoke to Gage, finger toggling between the four of them. "Don't worry. I won't be coming back for this one." The jerk of his chin pointed to Emma, and then James turned and stalked outside, Nicole following behind. Gage slammed the door so hard behind them that it rattled the walls of the house. A cry from Hudson quickly followed.

Gage pressed palms into his closed eyes. "I—"

"I'll check on him." Emma escaped down the hall and comforted Hudson. "It's okay, it's okay. You're all right. There won't be any more loud noises from us." She soothed a hand over his forehead, and his eyelids drooped. She repeated the motion as her mind whirled with the enormity of the exchange that had just taken place. Had Gage understood that comment from James? Even if he hadn't, she'd have to tell him the truth now. And break the renewed spirit that had risen up in him over the last month.

The parting shot from James would have implications that stretched far beyond today *if* Gage let the revelation break him. And this time, Emma didn't have enough faith to assure herself that it wouldn't.

Gage couldn't move. He hunched near the front door, attempting to steady his choppy breath. Nicole and James showing up had sent him into a state of shock. When he'd come out of Hudson's room to find Emma face-to-face with his past, Gage had wanted to dive in front of her. Shield her.

Instead, she'd supported him. The simple gesture of Emma holding his hand had given him the strength he'd needed.

Emma returned, and Gage didn't think, didn't analyze —he just strode to meet her, enveloping her, holding her tight against his chest. "I'm sorry I woke him, I just…" Lost it.

Emma peered up at him, her hand landing gently against his face. "He's fine. He went right back to sleep."

The fact that Nicole had mentioned the baby turned Gage's vision crimson. He would never let any harm come to Hudson. And of course Nicole had no case. No justification for any of her accusations. She was just lobbing bombs, hoping one would land and explode in just the right way that a windfall of cash would float in her direction.

When she'd first left with James, Gage had heard from a mutual acquaintance that the man had a knack for losing his shirt gambling. No doubt the money the two of them sought today would be to clear up his debts.

Emma didn't move from his embrace. Instead, she

tucked into him like she'd been meant for exactly that spot, somehow making the world right again.

"I'm so sorry, Em. Sorry you were here for that, that you had to witness…" His head shook. "I shouldn't have made you stay." Why had he? Because he'd needed her. Still, it had been selfish of him.

Her arms squeezed tight around his waist. "Stop apologizing, Counselor. You didn't do anything wrong."

He shuddered, fighting the urge to shower off and wash away that encounter like he would a day of ranching. Nicole had changed so much over time. But maybe this side of her had always been present and he hadn't realized it until they were already married.

She was a sad version of herself. Of who she could be.

After their divorce, Gage had let the aftermath of Nicole dictate his decisions.

No more.

He kissed the top of Emma's head, inhaling her sweet scent. "I can't believe I ever let her ruin my future. My faith. I let that hold me back from you and everything I kept hoping and trying not to hope might happen between us."

Emma glanced up, her eyes wide and…filling with tears? Were they the good kind? Or bad?

Her smile crested. "I'm so glad to hear you say that."

Relief nestled inside of him. "I don't deserve you, Emma. You taught me to live again."

"It was always in you. Someone just had to peel back a few layers."

"You."

"God and Hudson."

"All three of you."

Her cheeks crinkled. "That works." And then her

smile faded. "Gage, there's something I need to tell you. About what James said before he left."

He really didn't want to talk about James anymore. He wanted to kiss his girl. *His Emma.* Everything about her surprised him in the best way. Gage had never expected to have Emma in his life, but now he couldn't imagine it—any of it—without her.

He captured her lips, teasing, tasting, as if he had all of the time in the world. Because, suddenly, he did. A future that hadn't existed now stood a chance of being resurrected.

Emma melted against him, and he buried fingers in her hair, loosening her ponytail.

Interesting switch we've got going here. Don't worry. I won't be coming back for this one. The last statement by James slowed his exploration. What had the weasel meant by that?

Gage inched back. Emma's eyelids remained shuttered, her lips sporting evidence of his kiss.

A hum of contentment slipped from her throat. "When you do that, I can't think."

"That makes two of us." His lips lingered against her cheek, the corner of her mouth, the curve of her ear. "What do you need to tell me?"

Her face contorted, and for a second he thought he'd shifted and accidentally stepped on her toes. But then he realized her agony was emotional. "James was…" She swallowed, eyes open and pained now. "He was referring to the fact that he and I dated for a bit. Before he had anything to do with Nicole."

Gage went hot, then cold. If that were true, Emma would have told him. She was the most honest person he knew. She would never cheat or hide anything. Which was why he'd opened up to her.

Emma took his limp hand—he hadn't consciously let go of her, so it must have fallen of its own accord—and pressed a kiss to his knuckles, her attention sticking there. "I didn't tell you because we weren't an item, you and I. And I didn't think the opportunity for us to be would ever arise. Not with me wanting kids and you not. Plus, I wasn't sure if you could ever feel about me the way I do about you. I mean, you're way out of my league."

She was the one who was too pristine, too perfect for him. And yet, here she was, shattering that theory.

Earnest eyes held his. "I would have told you sooner if you'd ever asked me out. Or done more than kiss me and regret it." Her shoulders lifted. "But you didn't. So I kept my embarrassing secret to myself. James was a jerk, and I felt so stupid for having dated him at all. I wanted to feel loved. Noticed. And he made me feel that way at first." Her voice shook. "It took me a few weeks to realize he was fake. His words. His actions. Nothing about him was true."

Gage didn't want to believe it. Emma wouldn't hide something like that from him, would she? But she was admitting she had. His mind spun, and at the forefront was gut-wrenching, stepped-on-by-a-two-thousand-pound-bull pain.

"You didn't think it was important to tell me that you'd dated the man who stole my wife?"

Emma flinched. "Ex-wife. And, honestly, I was worried about you. Afraid that knowing would crush you and negate all of the ways you've softened and changed since Hudson's arrival."

"You should have said something right away." Before she'd let anything romantic develop between them. Gage's hand snaked to the back of his neck, where it felt like a boulder had been dropped from ten stories up. "How could you not tell me? I thought you were different. I thought—"

"I am!" Emma's voice sparked, and she grew a backbone right in front of him. "That relationship hurt me deeply, Gage. You have no right to demand that I should have shared it with you when up until just a few minutes ago, you did nothing but remind me that we had no chance for a future together." The wobble in her voice traveled to her body, but her tone was made of fire. "You know what I think?" Her finger poked into his chest. "I think I'm in love with you. I have been for a while. And I think..." She squared her shoulders. "You love me, too." Irritation vibrated from her. "You want to keep Hudson, but you let fear hold you back. And now you're using this stupid opportunity to run and hide. Guard yourself. So you can go back to your never-going-to-have-kids, don't-have-enough-faith-that-you-can-make-a-marriage-work cave. I think you love both of us, but you're just too afraid to reach out and take hold. So you go ahead and keep hiding behind your excuses. Keep living in the dark because you're afraid of the light."

She tore over to the closet and found her things, clenching her purse and coat in front of her as she faced him again. "You're deathly frightened, Gage. That's why you're blowing this hugely out of proportion. Because I did nothing wrong in not telling you about James. He was a sore point in my past. And had you reached out, had you asked anything about my dating history, then maybe I would have opened up about it. But you were too busy building fences between us, too busy tamping in immovable posts to really dive into me or my story. So you stay here with your self-righteousness to keep you company. I have better places to be."

The door clicked shut softly behind her—of course Emma would manage to corral her anger in order not to wake Hudson. But her words stayed behind to torment him. Leaving him hollow. Shattered.

Because his biggest fear was that she was right.

Chapter Fourteen

"Aunt Emma, do you think my picture is pretty?" Ruby held up a crayon drawing that included a lot of lines… and a zebra? Emma knew better than to guess at what it contained.

"It's about the most gorgeous piece of artwork I've seen all year." She pressed a kiss to her niece's head, feeling sentimental. "I love it."

Ruby beamed from her kneeling perch next to the lodge living room coffee table and concentrated on adding her name to the bottom corner, tongue slipping between her lips as she worked.

See? Emma didn't need Gage or Hudson or a family of her own. She'd just be the best aunt ever. On call for baby snuggles and teenage emergencies—like Ruby not getting along with her parents. And one day Mackenzie would meet her match, and then Emma could love her kiddos, too.

Maybe Emma's body would hurt less if she stopped wanting so much. Then her head would stop aching and her soul would numb itself.

That's what she needed to do—stop hoping.

But in the short time since she'd left Gage's and the encounter with James and Nicole, Emma had only managed not to cry.

She'd known she had to help out with the group this afternoon, so she'd battled tears like crazy on her drive home. After arriving at her cabin, she'd changed into her Wilder polo, jeans and boots and then pulled herself together.

"Emma." Luc came from upstairs, which functioned as a conference area, square dancing and multipurpose room. "The group is about to stop for their afternoon break. Do you have the snacks and drinks set out for them?"

Nope. But that *was* why she'd headed over to the lodge thirty minutes ago. Not to sit and color with Ruby. When she'd "pulled herself together" earlier, she must have forgotten her brain.

"I'll get right on it. How long until they break?"

"Five minutes. What have you been doing?"

She worried her lip. "Coloring?" No use in covering it up since the paper in front of her held plenty of evidence—two hands clenching a fistful of flowers. Come to think of it, the whole thing looked a bit too much like a simple bridal bouquet.

Emma crumpled the paper and stood. "Sorry. Not sure what I was thinking, but I'll get it taken care of." She jogged into the kitchen and started brewing regular and decaf, then filled a pot with hot water for tea.

Thankfully, the treats Joe had made earlier were already on platters and the table was up in the hallway outside of the dining room. She could whip things into shape quickly.

Hopefully.

Emma grabbed a tray of snacks from the stainless steel countertop and almost ran into her brother as she exited. "What are you doing?" Her voice snapped, and Luc's eyes flew wide.

"Helping. Are you okay?"

"Of course!" Her perky was broken, resulting in a cracked assurance, so Emma kept moving. She deposited the food and returned to the kitchen to retrieve the variations of sugar and fill a service carafe with creamer.

Her brother stacked napkins and small plates, working silently, questions he thankfully didn't ask brewing along with the coffee. So much for handling the afternoon break. They took shifts for a reason, and Emma had just majorly bombed on hers.

By the time they finished setting up, the group had already begun filtering out, using the restrooms. They'd gotten everything out in time—barely—thanks to Luc's help. The ladies—all in women's ministry—came downstairs, chatting, voices a level of happy Emma wasn't sure she could still access. A baby's cry rose above the hubbub. Agitated. Fussy.

Hudson?

Emma scanned the crowd. Was Gage here? Maybe he—or more likely Hudson—needed her.

She finally spotted the munchkin. A little girl with curls covering her head. Around six months old or so. She must have come with her mama for the day. Emma hadn't expected that. The girl continued to fuss as her mother took her into the lobby area. Probably to calm her without an audience watching.

Emma's ribs squeezed so tightly that passing out would be a relief. It hurt too much.

Despite the fact that she should stay and greet people,

watch the supplies and make sure everything went okay, Emma ran. Luc would handle it. He always did. Was she even needed around here?

The lobby had people in it, so Emma sought cover in the kitchen as the tears she'd penciled in for later broke loose. She'd planned to wait until after tonight's dinner to break down. Then she could hole up in her bathtub or bed and indulge in an ugly cry. But here? With all of the guests milling around? Horrible timing.

Emma strode to the back of the kitchen—past the stainless steel industrial counters—and dropped to a sitting position on the floor along the back wall shelving. She'd wait it out until the guests resumed their afternoon session. Then she could escape without bumping into anyone.

The door to the kitchen whooshed open, sound filtering inside and then fading. Emma resisted the urge to curl up in the fetal position and wish herself invisible. But no one would know she was back here.

"Emma?"

She winced. Cate. What was she doing over here? Before Emma could decide whether or not to answer, Cate rounded the countertop. "Oh, honey, what's wrong?" She sank to a sitting position by Emma's feet, stretching her legs out parallel, her shiny red flats the perfect exclamation point to her stylish jeans and white maternity shirt. Cate had bought the outfit online to tide her over until the two of them could go shopping. "Did something happen with one of the guests? I came over to grab Ruby, and Luc said you'd disappeared all of a sudden."

"I just needed a moment."

"On the kitchen floor?"

"You don't have to sit here with me. I have no doubt

it goes against everything in you to be sitting on an industrial kitchen floor." Cate wasn't much for germs. Or dirt. Or anything out of place.

"And I have no doubt Joe runs a tight ship. I'm sure this place has been bleached recently." Amusement creased her cheeks. "Or at least that's what I'm telling myself. And you're not getting rid of me that easily."

Except then Cate did push herself up. She rose on her tiptoes to reach the shelf above Emma and snagged a box of napkins. After ripping it open, she dropped a stack onto Emma's lap. Then she lowered herself to her previous position.

"Thank you for these." Emma picked up a napkin, wiped her tears and blew her nose. "I should get back out there. Help."

"Luc's out there. He'll host and clean up. You sit right here and take a minute. Or ten."

"I accused Gage of loving me." That was one way to spill the beans.

Cate's jaw unhinged. "I didn't know love was on the table. I thought we were still worried about you getting attached to Hudson."

Everything tumbled out of Emma, her feelings for Gage, The Kiss, the encounter with Nicole and James.

"So what happened after they left?"

Emma shut her eyes. Rubbed fingertips across her temples. "Gage told me he didn't want to let Nicole hold him back anymore. From me." That revelation had turned her inside out. If only he hadn't slipped through her fingers so fast. "And then he kissed me again." And what a kiss it had been, with Gage not holding back part of himself. But it had been short-lived. "And then I told Gage that I'd dated James once upon a time."

Recognition dawned. "So James was the one you told me about? The manipulative jerk?"

She nodded. "Never once did I think Gage would actually let us progress to anything more than friendship. If I had, I would have told him earlier. But I didn't think there was any hope until his declaration after they left. And that's not exactly the kind of news a girl takes out an ad in the paper for. I didn't share it with him because I was embarrassed. And when I did consider telling him, I was so afraid that it would send him backward. He's come so far, softened and changed so much since Hudson. I didn't want to wreck that. And that's exactly what happened. He was so upset."

Cate squeezed her shin through her jeans. "You weren't wrong not to tell him. Don't beat yourself up."

"I wish I hadn't been so weak as to have dated James in the first place."

"Oh, Emma. There is nothing weak about you. You dated the guy for how long?"

"About a month."

Cate waved away that amount of time as though it was nothing more than a pesky fly. "You can't know a person before you date them. And you barely did. Which means your instincts were spot on. And the minute God directed you, showing you that James wasn't right for you, you listened. You're so much stronger than you think. You broke up with him. Ended things quickly when you felt led to do exactly that. Emma, you're one of the strongest people I know."

Huh. Emma hadn't thought of it like that before. But still, the scene with Gage haunted her. "I lost it, Cate. I told Gage I thought he was in love with Hudson and me. *I accused him of loving me.*" Who did that? Emma wanted to slap a hand against her forehead. Or go back and do the same over her mouth. She still could not believe those words had tumbled out. She'd definitely gone and lost her mind. The first time in her life she'd freaked out to that extent, and it had to involve telling a guy that not only did she love him, but she was quite certain he loved her.

Instead of wearing shock, Cate's lips had morphed into an extra-large arch. And then she had the audacity to laugh. "Did you really?"

Emma nodded.

"That's the best thing I've heard in ages. Good for you, Em. Based on everything you've told me, including those kisses, it sounds like he is in love with you."

"Doubtful." Emma wanted the big kind of love. The kind where two people couldn't live without each other and would do anything to make it work. And since Gage hadn't called her after she'd left—hadn't texted—maybe his supposed feelings for her were the small kind.

She didn't even know if he was considering keeping Hudson or having kids one day. Their conversation hadn't gotten that far. But he wouldn't have admitted feelings for her if he hadn't changed his mind, would he?

Not that it mattered anymore.

"If he's not crazy about you, he's a fool. I can't think of anyone better than you to love. Why didn't I see this was happening before? How did I miss all of this? It must be pregnancy hormones."

"You didn't. Not really. It happened so fast. I didn't realize how far gone I was until this week. And then it was too late."

Cate sighed, sympathetic. "That is how it goes sometimes."

"Do you have any advice for me? Besides run and hide? I've got that part down pat."

"We could send Luc over there to talk some sense into him."

"Um, I'm going to go with *no*. Promise me you won't do that."

"I probably shouldn't make that promise since I'm not sure I can keep it."

Blerg. The last thing Emma needed was Luc getting involved.

The door to the kitchen opened, and by mutual silent agreement, neither of them spoke. The fridge opened, then shut. A *clank* sounded.

And then Emma sneezed. She tried to stop it. But as sneezes were apt to do in church or school or anywhere else one didn't want to be noticed, it loudly announced its arrival.

"Hello? Someone here?"

Mackenzie.

"Back here."

Mackenzie's head peeked around the corner. "Emma? Cate? What are you two doing?" Her eyes widened, landing on Cate. "Did you fall? I'll get Luc—"

"I'm fine!" Cate shooed away her concern. "We're just sitting here...talking."

"How is it out there?" Emma added. "Do they need help?"

"Ah." Kenzie glanced between the two of them sitting on the floor, confusion still evident. "No, they already went back up and Luc's leaving the snack out for a bit. We're not needed until dinner. I was just refilling my tea." Mackenzie lifted her glass as her stare narrowed, lips forming a bud. "Emma? What am I missing here?"

"I told Gage that I loved him this morning." Mackenzie's mouth dropped open. "And then I accused him of being in love with Hudson...and me."

"Whoa." Mackenzie deposited her tea on the countertop and then crossed over their legs in one long stride. She slid to a seat on the other side of Emma, stretching out so that the two women hemmed her in. Mackenzie, unlike Cate, probably didn't give a second thought to her jeans or boots or T-shirt meeting the floor. Her sister would roll in a mud puddle if an adventure was attached to it. "How did I miss all of this happening?"

"We all did," Cate raised her arms, exasperated.

"In your defense, I haven't been home much."

"You've been over at Gage's—" Mackenzie waggled her eyebrows "—watching Hudson." She made air quotes around the last two words.

Cate chuckled.

"You two are no help at all." But then Emma laughed, and it felt good. Like maybe her shriveled-up soul might make it through this mess intact.

"Things did not end well." Cate filled Mackenzie in.

Her sister placed a hand on her other leg and squeezed. "Sorry, sis. If he doesn't love you back, then he's an idiot."

"That's what I said!" Cate jumped in.

At least Emma would always have her girls on her side. "Well, I'm glad you two are in agreement, but unfortunately, it's too late. He thinks I betrayed him by not telling him about having dated James before Nicole did."

Mackenzie's face disclosed a second of surprise. "Is that who you were dating a couple of years ago? The mystery man who never came to pick you up?"

"Yep."

"Oh." Mackenzie winced.

"Exactly."

"Gage is upset with me, which I get, but his reaction made me so mad I'm not sure I even want to talk to him at this point." Lies. All lies. What Emma truly desired was for Gage to knock on her door and force a conversation between them. For both of them to understand where the other was coming from.

And then kisses and marriage and babies with the man.

In that order. Although with Gage, the baby would come first. And Emma was okay with that. She couldn't imagine her life without her two favorite guys in it. And yet, that nightmare had turned real and final after her altercation with Gage today.

"Did you lose it with Gage?" At Emma's nod, Mackenzie whooped and laughed. "That shows just how far gone you are. You never get upset at anyone for anything."

"That's not true."

"It is absolutely true."

The kitchen door opened. Again. Seriously? Emma rolled her eyes. This was turning into a game of sardines. Footsteps sounded, investigating, and then Luc stood over them, confusion splitting his forehead. "What's going—" He knelt to eye level with Cate. "Are you okay? Did something—"

"I'm fine." Her hand went up, landing gently on his cheek, reassuring. "Didn't fall. Not hurt."

His gaze swung to Emma and Mackenzie. "And the two of you are okay?"

For the most part. "Yes, we're fine," Emma answered. Luc stayed perfectly still, most likely waiting for them to fill him in. To explain why they were sitting on the floor in the kitchen.

No one did.

"Do I need to go rough someone up?"

They laughed.

"If that were necessary, I'd take care of it." Mackenzie quirked an eyebrow. "And these two would be with me."

True. The three of them could do some damage if needed. But it wasn't. Because it was too late to salvage any of it. And another attack on Gage like the one Emma had recently launched wouldn't help anything. He had to come to his own conclusions, whatever they might be.

"So no one's going to tell me what's going on?"

Emma dug up a smile. "Nope."

Luc's head shook. "As long as I live, I don't think I'll ever truly understand women." He stood. "We don't need to prep for dinner for a little while. So you three just—" he circled a hand over them "—finish up this strange little kitchen meeting you're having."

They laughed as he departed. Emma's ended on a hiccup, but it still felt good. See? She would be okay. Somehow.

Just maybe not tonight.

"Hello? Gage? You here?"

The call came from the other side of the barn, and Gage jerked the top half of his body out of the freezer he'd been cleaning, the smell of vinegar pungent.

"Back here." He'd been punishing himself with menial tasks this morning. Cleaning the deep freeze as if the success of the ranch depended on it. So far the chore had only allowed him the opportunity to turn what happened with Emma over and over in his mind. Nothing good could come of hashing out what had gone down between them.

Luc poked his head through the door to the area Gage was in. Ho-boy. Gage was half surprised his friend didn't come in swinging. Gage deserved it and more.

Only... Luc didn't seem upset.

"Hey, what's up?" And Gage's general statement should really be translated into *how's Emma*? It had almost killed him not to know how she'd been the last few days since the encounter with Nicole and James. The revelation that she'd dated that massive jerk. Gage's stomach twisted with suppressed anger at the idea of James being anywhere near Emma. Of not knowing they'd dated. And yet, the same question kept repeating. What did it matter?

He couldn't shake the memory of Emma's face when he'd gotten upset. It made him sick to think he'd hurt her. Again.

"That's what I came to ask you." Luc perched on a seesaw, and Gage tossed the rag into the vinegar cleaning bucket near his feet. "Any chance you can tell me why all of the women at the Wilder Ranch are acting strange? Because no one will tell me anything, and it's driving me nuts."

Gage searched for accusation behind Luc's question and didn't find any. So maybe he didn't know what had happened between Gage and Emma.

"How are they acting?"

"Weird. Ornery. Well, with Cate and Mackenzie, it's mostly mysterious. But Emma's miserable as all get-out. And that is not her normal mode of operation."

Great. Emma deserved so much more than Gage. Than all of his mistakes and failures. And just like he'd feared, they'd impacted her. Wounded her. He hated that the most.

"When I ask Cate what's going on, she says I need to talk to Emma."

The blood in his body dove to his feet, leaving a skittering, faint pulse behind.

"And when I ask Emma what's wrong, she won't say anything. She just tries to reassure me she's okay when she's obviously not. She's as sad as when her kitten Ariel died when we were kids, and I can't handle it another day. So I thought I'd see if you knew what was up."

Oh, pretty sure I just broke your sister's heart, that's all. Gage kept going back to when Emma had said she loved him. *Loved him.* Gage deserved every accusation she'd lobbed his way. And Emma had been right. He had fallen for Hudson. For her. Gage didn't want to give either of them up, but he wasn't sure how to reconcile that with what he'd believed for so long.

He leaned back against the deep freeze, squeezing the lid. "Emma didn't show up to watch Hudson this morning. Sent a high school girl over. A homeschooler she knows."

Luc's eyes narrowed. "I heard that, too, and that was after she wouldn't go to church yesterday. Stayed home like she's sick. But I don't think she is."

Lovesick. Heartsick. And the blame all went to Gage.

"That's what sent me sniffing over here. Wondering what you know that I don't."

Here it came. The big-brother protection. Well, Luc didn't have to tell Gage that he wasn't good enough for his little sister. Gage already knew. Had figured that out right away.

What was Gage supposed to say? Where should he start? "It's all my fault." As good a place as any.

"Why? What does Emma's upset have to do with you?"

"We had an—" altercation? "—interaction with Nicole and James on Saturday."

Luc's jaw went slightly ajar. "They came here?"

Gage nodded. "Emma answered the door. Things were said. I found out Emma had dated James before Nicole did."

"What?" The snap in Luc's tone told Gage he hadn't been the only one not to know. "She dated that jerk? Did he do anything to her when they came by? Say something to upset her?" Luc's fists turned white. "If he did—"

"It wasn't James that upset her." Nope. Gage had handled that all on his own. Emma must really have been embarrassed by her relationship with James not to have told him about it. And, as she'd said, she hadn't wanted him to backpedal at the revelation.

With someone else that might sound like an excuse. But not with Emma. She would truly care about the impact news like that would have on him.

Everyone had a skeleton or two in their closet they didn't want anyone to uncover. And yet, Gage had torched Emma for hers. Driven in the knife and twisted. He could add it to his unforgivable list.

"Then what did?"

Me. All me. "Can we have this conversation with you acting as my friend instead of Emma's brother?"

"Ahh, okay. Why do I get the feeling I'm not going to like where this is headed?"

"You might not." Gage swallowed. He needed to get this stuff off his chest. Talk to someone. And after losing Zeke, Luc was the closest friend he had. He was tired of hiding his mistakes. Might as well fan them out in the open and take the punishment that fit the crime.

"After James and Nicole left, Emma told me about dating James. And I got upset with her for not telling me about it earlier. I thought she'd hidden it from me. But now I realize why she didn't say anything. She was embarrassed she'd dated him. And probably didn't want to bring him up around me."

"Understandable."

"Right. But when I got mad, Emma… Well, she lost it. She defended herself. And then she accused me of having feelings for her. And Hudson. She said that I loved them and I wouldn't admit it."

"Emma did…said…all of that?" Surprise registered on Luc's mug, and then he threw his head back and laughed. Deep. Loud. "Oh, that is good. You're in a heap of trouble, man."

Gage resisted the strangest urge to smile as emotion built behind his eyes. If there was one good thing that had come out of his stupidity, it was Emma verbally kicking his behind. He'd always known she had it in her. That she was as strong as she was sweet. He just wished it hadn't surfaced in his direction. Even though he'd deserved it.

"Do you…have feelings for her?" Luc choked in the middle of his sentence, and Gage thought his next words might earn him that punch he'd expected earlier.

"What would you say if I did?" His voice was made of gravel. "Because I don't deserve her."

"No one deserves Emma. She's—"

"Sunshine. Everything and everyone she comes into contact with is better because of her."

A confused, slow smile eased over Luc's countenance. "If you know that, then you've got it figured out. I can't believe you love my sister."

"I didn't say I loved her."

Luc raised an eyebrow. A sigh-groan ripped from Gage. "Okay, I do. But I don't know what to do with that. I'm sure you can understand that she's so innocent and I'm so…" Used. Worn. Lacking in hope and faith. "I'm sure you'd rather not see your sister end up with someone like me."

"That's a lot of *sures*. Especially since I don't think you're a mind reader. But yeah, I'm *sure* you're right. Why would I want my sister to end up with a guy like you? A hard worker. Someone who believes in God. Who sees Emma for the gift she is and loves her. And not only that, from what you're telling me, she loves you." Luc's tone dripped with sarcasm. "Right. I can see how I'd not want that for Emma."

"Okay, now I need Emma's brother to come back. Because he'll understand that I'm not worthy of her. I have baggage. A divorce under my belt."

Luc's brow wrinkled. "When I look at you, I don't see your past. I see you. Just the man you are. And if that guy loves my sister…"

"I do." Gage said it with more conviction than he'd allowed himself up until this point. Because it was true. He loved Emma. Probably had from the first moment she'd climbed into the back seat with Hudson and become his biggest cheerleader. The one who believed in him more than he believed in himself. Emma wouldn't have any doubts that he could make a marriage work. She loved him. She didn't care about who he'd been. His mistakes.

And when he saw himself through her eyes, Gage just might be able to start believing again, too.

Or, at least he could have. Before he'd botched it all up. Who knew how Emma felt about him now.

"I don't have a problem with you being in her life. With you dating Emma. Not if that's what she wants. Did you think I would?"

Relief crept in, and Gage scrubbed a hand through his hair. "Maybe. Or maybe it was all me. My issues. I thought you'd see me through the lens of my mistakes."

"If Cate hadn't given me a chance to prove to her that I'm a different man now than I was at twenty, I wouldn't have her or Ruby here full-time. Or twins on the way. I'm not holding your divorce against you or keeping score. And I don't think you should, either. Your fears were unfounded."

Gage wanted to curl into a ball, hole up in the corner of the portable crib like Hudson and wail and kick and scream. Because he was figuring all of this out too late. "She was so upset with me. Have you ever seen Emma lose it?"

"Once or twice. It's pretty rare."

Gage would laugh at the picture of Emma giving him the what for if it wasn't so disheartening. "She's done with me. Why would she ever give me a chance after the way I treated her?"

"If I know Emma, and I think I do, you've got a strong chance of winning her over. She's… Emma."

"Maybe." But Gage wasn't so sure. "Up until Emma, I didn't think that I'd ever get married again. Was adamant that I didn't want kids. And then she showed up and turned everything upside down. Her and Hudson."

Which reminded Gage that before he could even attempt to win Emma back, to convince her to give him a chance, he had a baby situation to figure out.

"I'm meeting this afternoon with the missionaries who are interested in adopting Hudson. And in the last few days, I haven't been able to stop thinking about keeping him myself. That was never the plan. But the idea of giving up Zeke's kid when he entrusted him to me… I don't know if I can. So what am I supposed to do now? Tell them that maybe I'm supposed to keep him all of a sudden? But that I'm still not sure? I've been praying nonstop, but God hasn't hit me over the head with an answer. I want the best for Hudson, and I'm just not sure that's me. How am I supposed to know for sure?"

Luc's breath leaked out, loud. His hand snaked to the back of his neck. Not exactly a confidence builder. "I don't know. But I can pray. I'll pray the answer is clear. That God makes the fleece wet for you."

The reference to Gideon in Judges made Gage smile for the first time in days. Yes, he could use a wet fleece and a dry threshing floor. And then a dry fleece and wet threshing floor. And then a third, just to be sure.

"Thanks. I appreciate it."

"'Course. About time I could be your sounding board. You were mine after Cate showed up. And then left. And I don't regret fighting for her one bit."

His words held a message that lodged in Gage's chest. Deep. Sure. Maybe it was time to move past what had happened with Nicole. To know she'd played her part in their demise. And he'd played his. He could accept that, move forward and do things differently the next time. With Emma—if she'd have him.

But first he had to figure out what to do about Hudson.

Chapter Fifteen

A text notification sounded from her phone as Emma stapled the letter *W* of next summer's theme to the bulletin board on the wall in the Kids' Club—a cabin that had been renovated years earlier and was now used solely for the program.

She checked her phone. It was from her brother. There's a package for you at the lodge.

Huh. Likely supplies she'd ordered for the summer, though if so, they'd arrived early.

Since she was close to done, Emma added the *i*, *l*, and *d* to the *Adventure in the Wild* summer theme. It was a play off their last name, of course, but also a way to incorporate animals into the program. She didn't teach during Kids' Club, but she liked to have a purpose. A focus.

Much like she did in life. But in the last couple of days Emma had been drifting. She hadn't gone to Gage's to watch Hudson yesterday or today. It had taken most of her strength not to march over there, steal that baby and bring him home to her cabin for the time being. Because she just couldn't see Gage right now. Even if it meant losing out on time with her little man.

Emma had called a homeschool family from church and asked if one of their older girls could watch Hudson for a few days. Just until she found her bearings again. Until she could see Gage without losing her mind, crying or engaging in another one-sided shouting match. Because, yeah, she was still upset about how everything had gone down. And she still loved him. Unfortunately, those feelings hadn't gone away. Which just made all of this harder, because she missed him.

She missed her two favorite guys.

"Enough." Emma threw her hands into the air with a groan. "I'm so done with feeling this way."

She tossed the stapler she'd been using onto the small table surrounded by equally small chairs. She'd go check out the package.

The walk over to the lodge was more bitter than she'd expected. Bright sunshine didn't impact the temperature, which sat squarely in the midthirties. And Emma hadn't thought to wear a jacket. Only a sweatshirt. Gage's, to be exact.

This morning when she'd gotten dressed, it had called out to her from the chair in the corner of her room. She'd worn it home accidentally last week, and then had conveniently forgotten to return it to Gage in the days after.

A little like a high school girl stealing her boyfriend's jersey. But then, Emma couldn't call Gage that, could she? Even an ex-boyfriend was a stretch, because they'd never made it that far.

She buried her nose in the shoulder, inhaling everything Gage—a hint of outdoors, his intoxicating fragrance of lotion or whatever made him smell like a yummy men's cologne sample. Yep, she definitely missed him.

He hadn't contacted her once since the James/Nicole

fiasco. No text or phone call. He hadn't shown up on her step. Nada.

Emma entered the lodge and paused in the doorway to the front office. Luc's was at the end of the hall, so if the package wasn't in here, he likely had it in his office.

She spied two medium-sized boxes perched on the first desk that was currently empty and would be filled come summer. A cup of iced tea was on Mackenzie's desk, which meant she must be in the lodge somewhere.

Emma scrounged for scissors and then slit open the first box. She removed the packing material and peered underneath. What in the world? The book on top was on her wish list, but she hadn't purchased it. The one underneath was also one she wanted but hadn't bought yet. And the stack continued. Emma tore into the second box, finding the same. There must be thirty books between the two packages.

Had she clicked a buy button by accident? One that would purchase the whole list? She couldn't imagine that was the case. A packing slip was in the bottom of the second box.

There was an order date—last Thursday—and a note in the memo section.

Emma, nothing will ever be enough to thank you for all you've done and how you've cared for Hudson. —G

Gage? He'd done this. But how? Emma sank into the chair behind the desk and it rolled backward. Last week Cate had asked to borrow Emma's phone when they'd been hanging out. She'd thought it strange but had assumed her reception wasn't great or her battery close to dead. But she must have been spying, copying Emma's book wish list and sending it off to Gage.

Total Judas-in-the-Garden-of-Gethsemane move. Only maybe not quite that extreme.

Cate was under a deadline or Emma would trek over to the house right now and pepper her with questions. A smile toyed with her mouth as she slipped her phone from her pocket and texted instead.

He bought me books? How am I supposed to not fall in love with him now?

But, oh, how she'd already fallen. It was too late not to love him. Emma knew that full well.

I know. I almost cried when he asked me to get him a list. Forgive me?

As if there was anything to be forgiven. Of course!

And it was just that easy…with Cate. If only Gage would contact her and say something—anything—about Saturday. They really needed to discuss what had happened. But Emma refused to make the first move. Especially after she'd let her mouth run off like she had.

Was Gage still upset with her for not telling him that she'd dated James?

Emma could see his point. But she'd wanted so badly not to send him spiraling when he'd come so far back to the land of the living. And yet, her omission had done exactly that anyway.

Emma cradled a stack of the books to her chest. This man who'd sent her books, who noticed everything about her and cared for her like no one else did… She still harbored the faintest hope that he loved her. That maybe she'd been right to accuse him of it. Of course she could have gone about it all in a much different manner. But she couldn't help thinking that she knew him. Knew who he was in his heart and soul. Maybe even better than he knew himself.

"This is who he is." She spoke to the empty office. "Why can't he see that?" Why did Gage only recognize his faults when he looked in the mirror?

And who am I? Emma had wanted Gage to change, to open up all of this time, but she hadn't held herself to the same standard of transformation. She'd tucked away her ideas for the ranch because she was scared to fail. To be the meek little sister who was a dreamer and came up with out-of-touch concepts.

She had to talk to Luc and Mackenzie about her suggestions for the ranch. Because while Emma wasn't sure if Gage was going to follow through on changing, she was.

Before she lost her resolve, Emma strode down to Luc's office. She knocked, then poked her head inside. "Do you have a minute?"

"Of course." He stacked some papers. Studied her. "You okay, Em?"

She perched on the corner of his desk. "I think so. Or at least I'm going to be."

Brotherly concern stayed present in the squint of his eyes.

"You know those two outbuildings beyond the barn? Full of storage?"

"Yep."

"I think we should make them into an ice cream parlor and a store." Once she started talking, Emma didn't stop. She explained it all. When Mackenzie came in partway through and sat on the futon, listening, she kept going. She spilled everything. Outlined how they could remodel affordably. And then after it had all trickled out, she waited.

Luc and Mackenzie exchanged a look that Emma couldn't decipher. "It's annoying when you two communicate without words."

Luc laughed. "I was just wondering if Mackenzie thought it was as good of an idea as I do."

Emma glanced between them. "And?"

"I think it's great." Mackenzie pushed up from the futon and studied an old picture of the ranch that included one of the buildings. "We could make a patio right here." She pointed to the photo. "Add some pavers. Maybe a few tables with umbrellas. A place for families to hang out in the evening. We could even do some of the weekly shows down there, weather permitting. Maybe build a small outdoor stage. Switch things up."

Luc leaned back in his chair. "Em, how long have you been thinking about all of this?"

"Couple of weeks." She swallowed. *Strong and confident. No more meek.* "A bit longer, actually."

"Why didn't you say anything?" Mackenzie asked.

Emma pressed teeth into her lip, shoulders lifting. "I don't know. Guess I convinced myself it was fanciful. Impractical."

"It's not," Luc interjected. "Wish you would have said something earlier so we could have had it done for this summer."

The three of them brainstormed the store. Who in town made local products that they could sell. What items they could add the ranch logo to.

Why had Emma assumed that her siblings wouldn't listen to her? It was something about them being older—and twins, close ones—that had messed with her over the years. Oh, she'd known that they loved her and that she loved them.

But respect? Yeah, maybe she'd struggled with believing that they valued her. Looked up to her like she did to them even though she was younger.

After a few more minutes of discussion, Mackenzie headed down the hall and back to her work. Emma dropped onto the futon that faced Luc's desk. She was still reeling a little.

"Nice sweatshirt."

Oh. Right. She glanced down to where Luc's nod had landed.

"Have you talked to him?"

Emma's mouth dried as quickly as parched grass in a summer drought. "Cate told you?"

"No." He leaned forward, elbows on his desk, brotherly concern in place. "Gage did."

Gage had talked to Luc? When? What had been said? Emma felt like her laundry had been hung out on a clothesline for a bunch of ranch guests to see.

"Em…"

Luc's tone spooked her. "What? Is something wrong?" Was Hudson okay? Fists wrung her stomach like a sopped rag.

"Gage met with the missionary family yesterday afternoon about Hudson."

No. Gage was giving Hudson up? After everything? Emma felt like kicking something. And then drowning herself in a pint of Talenti Fudge Brownie Gelato.

Gage could absolutely raise Hudson on his own. He would be a wonderful father. Scratch that—not *would be.* Gage already was a dad to Hudson. He just didn't see it somehow.

But if Gage didn't believe in himself, then maybe he wasn't meant to raise Hudson. Perhaps a two-parent family would be better.

Emma shattered at the thought. Had she been wrong all of this time?

Either way, at least Emma had to say goodbye. She couldn't let Hudson go without holding him one more time. Without pressing another kiss to that sweet, soft head of hair.

She pushed up from the couch. "I've gotta go."

"Emma, wait."

She didn't stay to listen to her brother. Didn't slow down. Didn't want to hear what he had to say next even though it would probably be much more logical than her current state of mind.

Emma didn't have time to waste.

Gage's pulse hammered and skipped as he checked out the front window. Emma. Right on time.

When she'd texted earlier today asking to stop by and say goodbye to Hudson, Gage had suggested she come around six. He'd wanted to be home when she arrived.

Her hesitancy had shown through in her delayed reply text, but amazingly, she'd agreed. He'd spent the rest of the afternoon contemplating what to say to her and how to say it. Short of lassoing Emma, he couldn't force her to listen.

But he'd prayed that she would.

When he'd gotten back to the house, he'd been shocked to find out that she hadn't ditched their set time and shown up earlier to see Hudson in order to avoid him.

Gage had already sent the babysitter home. Showered.

Dressed in jeans and an untucked green button-down shirt. Paced a line in the wood floors.

Now he deposited Hudson in his play saucer and tore down the hallway. He got to his bedroom window in time to see Emma approach the front door. And then she disappeared from his line of vision.

But he could imagine her face as she saw the envelope bearing her name taped to the door. By now she'd be ripping it open, reading the first message.

You were right about everything. And she was. Including that he wanted to keep Hudson…and that he loved her.

He'd put three note cards into the envelope. The second simply said *I'm sorry.* The apology couldn't be more heartfelt.

And the third? *Come inside and stop standing out in the cold.*

Gage thought he heard her faint laughter as the front door opened. "Gage? Are you here?"

And now came the clincher. He'd stationed Hudson's saucer near the coffee table so that she'd see the additional envelope there. Gage had written in a messy, childlike scrawl on that note. *Emma, the only mom I want is you. —H*

He'd drawn stick figure parents holding hands with a child in the middle of them. Cheesy? Perhaps. But he didn't care what anyone else thought. Only Emma.

Gage inched out of his door and stealthily moved down the hallway. Emma had Hudson in her arms. She was cooing and talking to him. She kissed his head while holding the last note in her shaking hand, confusion and maybe a bit of hope residing on her features.

"It's all true." He walked slowly in her direction. "You

were right. I do love you, Emma Wilder. I'm crazy, out-of-my-mind in love with you. And I was too afraid to admit it. To take a leap and trust that our relationship had a future."

A glint of moisture coated her pretty steel-blue eyes that he'd missed so much over the past few days. She wore brown ankle boots, jeans and a navy-and-white-striped shirt, her hair pulled back in a messy bun with russet wooden earrings dangling. Hudson latched on to one, and Emma removed it from her ear. The second earring followed.

"What was I thinking, Sir Hudson? I forgot your infatuation with these things." She slipped them into her back pocket, attention returning to Gage. She held up the last note, a wobble in her grip. "What does this mean?"

No doubt Emma had plenty of questions for him, but Gage had been hoping for a better response to his admission. Maybe an *I love you, too.* Or still.

A corner of the paper in Emma's hand was missing, and since Hudson was currently gumming something, Gage stuck a finger into his mouth and dug it out. It wasn't like Emma to miss a detail like that. He took the note from her and wiped the slobbered piece onto it, then dropped the paper onto the coffee table. Brushed off any remaining dampness against his jeans.

"I met with the Franks yesterday."

Emma shuddered, hurt flitting across her beautiful face. "I heard that from Luc."

Thankfully, her brother hadn't filled her in completely. "I couldn't shake the feeling that I was supposed to keep Hudson. That finding another family wasn't right anymore. But I didn't know how to handle the Franks. The meeting had been set up for weeks—while they're stateside. I talked to Luc about it, and we both prayed that I'd know what to do. That the answer would be clear."

Relief ignited as the meeting replayed. God had certainly come through with flying colors. The fleece had been wet and dry and then some. "The Franks had been praying about adopting Hudson. They have three children already, but Mrs. Frank's doctor advised her not to carry another pregnancy. She had complications the last time. But every time they prayed, they both felt that they weren't supposed to adopt Hudson." Mr. Frank had described it as a resounding no. "They believed God was telling them that Hudson was already where he was supposed to be."

Emma's hand flew over her mouth, and then she sagged a little, the arm holding Hudson inching toward her hip.

Gage took the baby from her and moved him into the living room, wanting Emma all to himself for a minute. He surrounded Hudson with a few favorite toys and his sippy cup, but the boy crawled over to the movie cupboard and began unloading DVDs, chewing on them, then tossing them into a haphazard pile. Fine by Gage. Hudson could disorganize whatever he wanted as long as he didn't injure himself.

Gage returned to face Emma, his nervousness reaching bar-exam levels.

"So…you're keeping him?"

He couldn't decipher if her face held hope or simply shock.

He nodded. "You were right all along. I can't give him up. I still don't feel qualified to raise him, but that doesn't mean God won't equip me." Gage paused. Scrounged for courage. "I want you, too, Emma. In my life first and foremost, but Hudson's, too. But even if it's too late for that, I'm still keeping him. Even if I'm meant to do this on my own."

Tears spilled, tracking down her cheeks, and Gage stepped closer, catching the moisture with his thumbs. She didn't shrink from his touch. "Em, don't cry. I'm so sorry I hurt you. That I didn't believe in us. But it wasn't you that caused my lack of confidence. It was me. Always me. I thought I'd messed up too much the first time around and didn't deserve a second chance. And maybe I don't. But I want one. With you. I'm ready to believe that things can be different this time." *Can?* "Will be. Because you, Emma Wilder, are the best thing that has ever happened to me. And I don't want to go another day without you in my life. I want to marry you. I want you forever."

Nothing like putting it all on the line. But Gage would never forgive himself if he didn't. Still, his heart thrashed like a fresh catch on a dry dock as he waited for Emma to speak. But she still didn't. More moisture saturated her cheeks. *Oh, Emma.* What if he was too late? And he'd hurt Emma beyond repair? His need for her wasn't about Hudson. Gage now felt confident that God would provide for the two of them if they were to be a family. But he didn't want to move forward without Emma. Couldn't imagine not having sunshine again after so many years of cloud cover. Gage retrieved the tissues and offered them to her.

She blew her nose. Wiped under her eyes. "I think maybe we should start with a date before we head down the aisle." Her smile grew, and then she laughed.

The rubber band that had tightened around Gage's chest broke free. He crushed her against him. He actually felt her melt. Let go. As if she'd been holding herself together, too.

"I'm so sorry I hurt you. I'm going to try not to do that again."

"Okay." Her reply was muffled against his chest, arms banding around his waist.

"But I might." He shifted enough to see her face but didn't let go. "I need you to tell me if I do. To always be honest with me. Because I don't want to mess this up. I need to know so I can fix it if something's wrong."

"Okay." Softness radiated from her. "I might mess up, too. The deal goes both ways."

"I can't imagine that."

"Me, either." Teasing danced in her tone, her eyes.

His hands slid to cradle her face. "A date sounds really good, by the way." To go out to dinner with Emma, watch a movie with her, to hold her hand and kiss her and have it all be right and good…oh, yeah. He wanted that. "But just so we're clear, I'm not playing games. And I'm definitely not James. I know what I want, Emma, and it's you. That's not going to change."

Emma put her hands over his, capturing him. Holding him there. As if he wanted to go—be—anywhere else. "I feel the same way. You're stuck with me, Counselor. Both of you. Because I'm not going anywhere." His relief was so swift it buckled his knees. "I love you. So much." Finally, the words he'd been craving.

"I can promise you it's not as much as I love you. As I need you." Gage could guarantee that. He dropped his forehead to hers. "I was so afraid I was too late. That I'd messed it all up and that you wouldn't be able to forgive me. I should never have gotten upset about the James stuff. It doesn't matter. He doesn't matter. And I totally understand why you didn't say anything earlier."

"You do?"

"Yes. We don't ever have to talk about it again as far as I'm concerned."

"Sounds good to me."

He kissed her then, taking his time, tasting that plump lower lip that *owned* him. Kissing Emma was like walking into a candy store as a ten-year-old and being told he could pick out whatever he wanted, no parental limits involved. "Your lips have been driving me crazy for weeks now."

"Really?" Why did she sound so astonished?

"Really." Gage would have to spend the next fifty years convincing Emma just how stunning and amazing and mesmerizing she was. And he was just fine with that. "So, Emma Wilder, will you go on a date with me?"

She gave a shy, sweet grin. Nodded.

"Do you have a group at the ranch this Friday?"

Her head shook.

"I'll get a sitter for Hudson."

Her mouth formed a tight bud. "Maybe we should just hang out here. I don't really want to leave Hudson. I've missed him so much the last few days."

Spoken like a true mother. And that's what Emma was to Hudson. Maybe she didn't have the title yet, but she carried a banner that claimed him loud and clear. The little guy didn't know how good he had it with a mom like Emma in his future.

"There will be plenty of Hudson time to come. He's not going anywhere. And I want you all to myself for a night."

"Okay." Her exhale mingled with amusement and another dash of watery emotion.

The next question he asked quietly, near her ear. "And how about the week after that?" Emma stretched her neck to give him better access, and Gage grinned, dropping a kiss there.

"Mmm-hmm." She sounded breathless, distracted. Gage was just fine with that, too.

"And the one after that?"

Her bubbly laugh rang out. "You can have all of my days, Counselor. You pretty much already do."

"That—" he preoccupied her with another kiss "—is exactly what I wanted to hear."

Epilogue

Two perfect months, and then three days that made her doubt it all.

"I'm afraid Gage is going to break up with me." The statement spilled from Emma as Cate drove them home from their Denver shopping excursion. Baby supplies this time. The two of them had shopped for hours, stopped for lunch, then went at it some more. It had been the perfect distraction for Emma. But now that they neared home, the fears she'd been holding under water all day boiled to the surface, demanding her attention.

"What in the world would make you think that?"

"A week ago I would have said the idea of him breaking up with me was ludicrous. But he's been acting so strange the last few days. Mumbling to himself. Turning his phone so I can't see the screen when I go anywhere near it. As if I want to read his messages. I don't." Emma huffed. "Or at least I hadn't until he started hiding them." She twisted her hands together, her voice shifting into low gear. "I just can't shake the suspicion that something is wrong. Off. He canceled on me coming over last night without any real explanation. And when I told him I was going shopping with you today, he practically gave me a stack of bills to spend and a shove out the door." A forlorn sigh escaped as the familiar ranch drive came into view and Cate turned. "Like he was excited to be rid of me for the day."

Cate patted Emma's leg, the warmth a flash through her jeans. Emma had worn an oatmeal front-cross sweater today and her leather booties. Because sometimes a cute pair of boots made the messy parts of life more bearable.

"Hmm." Cate was definitely assuming the calmer role out of the two of them. "I bet he's just stressed about the ranch or even Hudson."

"Could be." But why the sudden change in his demeanor? The past two months had been sprinkled with gold fairy dust. As close to perfect as it got. Emma and Gage spent so much time together that Luc and Kenzie teased her about it on a daily basis. Love had turned her starry-eyed for sure, so she accepted the ribbing without complaint. Emma had thought that she'd been crazy in love with Gage back when he'd first decided to keep Hudson. But those feelings had only grown with time. At least for her. And up until this week, she'd thought they had for him, too.

Cate pulled up to the lodge and turned off the car. "I can say without a doubt that Gage loves you. That hasn't changed." A reassuring grin flashed. "I have to run inside to grab something for Luc out of his office. If you could come with me that would be great. I'll need your help carrying it."

"Sure." Emma unbuckled, and they walked up the lodge steps. It was dark inside, and she shook off the peculiar sense that someone or something was in the room with them. She flipped on the lights, and a cheer came from the group of people filling the lodge lobby.

Cate stood to Emma's side, her shrug mischievous. "I wasn't allowed to say anything."

So many of Emma's friends were present. And her parents. Her mom was holding Hudson, beaming at her. The room was decorated in various tones of teal and peppered with colorful tissue paper balls. Someone switched on white twinkle lights, illuminating an artfully designed table dripping with appetizers and desserts.

And right in the middle of everyone was Gage. He approached her, those crinkly eyes in full force, got down on one knee in front of her and produced a ring box.

Oh. Oh, my. A jet-engine roar started in Emma's ears.

"Emma Wilder, I cannot imagine my life without you." Adoration filled his voice, his gaze. "You are the best thing that has ever happened to me. Marry me, please? I'm not whole without you."

Was that squeal-like animal sound coming from her? Somewhere along the line, her hands had covered her mouth. Now she peeled them away. Forced her voice box into coherent functioning mode.

"I thought you were breaking up with me." *Seriously, Emma Wilder? The man you love is down on his knee and that's the gibberish that comes out of your mouth?*

"What?" Gage's head tilted and the ring box dipped, almost falling out of his grip. "Why would you think that?"

"You acted so weird the last few days, and I just got worried."

"Em." His grin grew, warming her from head to toe. "It's a lot of pressure and planning to propose to the most romantic woman I know. Organize all of these people."

His head jutted back to the crowd watching them with curiosity. "Hide your parents. Mine couldn't come but we Skyped them in."

She couldn't believe he'd done all of this. No wonder he'd been jumpy. Floundering for answers at the simplest inquiry. Now it all made sense.

"Any chance you're going to answer now?" Gage jiggled the ring box like one might dangle a bottle in front of a baby.

Her laugh was layered with the good, *is this really happening to me?* kind of tears.

"I will definitely marry you." And then she flew into his arms, practically tackling him to the ground. Gage managed to steady them both. He cradled her face with his free hand. His kiss was short and sweet, but the message traveled down to her toes.

"I love you, Emma. So much."

"I love you, too." She stole another kiss, then threw her hands above her head with a victory whoop. "I'm going to marry this man!" Their friends and family erupted in laughter and cheers.

Emma untangled herself from Gage and they both stood. He took the ring from the box and slid it onto her left ring finger. A princess-cut diamond sparkled back at her.

"You did good, Counselor."

He grinned, then swept her up in an embrace, his voice quiet, near her ear. "I can't believe you're going to be all mine for the rest of our lives."

"Me, either." A subdued screech of excitement escaped at the thought of Gage being her husband, her best friend, Hudson's father. Forever and ever, amen.

He lowered her reluctantly as family and friends approached, surrounding them, offering congratulations and waiting for hugs. "Guess I have to share you now."

"Yep." Her mouth battled to stay stoic, serious. "I actually have plans tonight."

A shadow of uncertainty crossed Gage's handsome face. "And what are those?"

She shot him a playful grin before turning to embrace her mom. "I have an engagement party to attend."

* * * * *

*If you enjoyed this story,
pick up these other books by Jill Lynn:*

Falling For Texas
Her Texas Family
Her Texas Cowboy
The Rancher's Surprise Daughter

Available now from Love Inspired!

Find more great reads at www.LoveInspired.com

Dear Reader,

I recently had to make a decision I was incredibly torn about, and I prayed earnestly that I would know what to do. I didn't receive a big sign like Gage, though I have had those appear in my life. This time God's answer was quiet. Hard to hear. Once I believed I understood His directive, I obeyed, even though it wasn't the answer I wanted. After, I felt overwhelming peace. And in the time since, that peace has remained whenever that particular situation comes to mind.

Regrettably, I don't always listen to God's leading. I try to do things my own way, or I fight the path He's directing me down. But the good news is, God never gives up on any of us. He loves us every step of the journey, whether we're stumbling to follow His plan or running a straight line in the right direction. He's consistent even when we're not, and I'm so thankful for that.

I'm also thankful for your support as readers. Your encouragement means the world. Thanks for celebrating book news with me and participating in the development of these stories. Hudson and Ford both earned their names from your suggestions.

I love to connect with readers. Sign up for book news and giveaways at www.Jill-Lynn.com/news or find me on social media: www.facebook.com/JillLynnAuthor & www.Instagram.com/JillLynnAuthor.

Jill Lynn

COMING NEXT MONTH FROM
Love Inspired®

Available February 19, 2019

THE AMISH BACHELOR'S BABY
Amish Spinster Club • by Jo Ann Brown

Finally following his dreams of opening a bakery, Caleb Hartz hires Annie Wagler as his assistant. But they both get more than they bargain for when his runaway teenage cousin and her infant son arrive. Can they work together to care for mother and child—without falling in love?

THE AMISH BAKER
by Marie E. Bast

When his son breaks one of baker Sarah Gingerich's prized possessions, widower Caleb Brenneman insists the boy make amends by doing odd jobs in her bake shop. While the child draws them together, can they ever overcome their differing Amish beliefs and become the perfect family?

RANCHER TO THE RESCUE
Three Brothers Ranch • by Arlene James

Coming to the aid of a woman in her broken-down car, Jake Smith doesn't expect to find the answer to his childcare problems. But Kathryn Stepp needs a job and the widower needs a nanny for his son. And their business arrangement might just develop into so much more.

HER LAST CHANCE COWBOY
Big Heart Ranch • by Tina Radcliffe

With a new job at Big Heart Ranch, pregnant single mom Hannah Vincent is ready for a fresh start. But as she and her boss, horse trainer Tripp Walker, grow closer, Hannah can't help but wonder if she's prepared for a new love.

HIS SECRET DAUGHTER
by Lisa Carter

When ex-soldier Jake McAbee learns he has a daughter, he's determined to raise the little girl. But can he win his daughter's trust and convince Callie Jackson—the child's foster mother—that the best place for Maisie is with him?

SEASON OF HOPE
by Lisa Jordan

Jake Holland needs a piece of land for his farming program for disabled veterans—but his ex-wife owns it. So they strike a deal: she'll sell him the land if he renovates her home. But can they resolve their past—and long-kept secrets—for a second chance?

———————

LOOK FOR THESE AND OTHER LOVE INSPIRED BOOKS WHEREVER BOOKS ARE SOLD, INCLUDING MOST BOOKSTORES, SUPERMARKETS, DISCOUNT STORES AND DRUGSTORES.

LICNM0219

Get 4 FREE REWARDS!

We'll send you 2 FREE Books plus 2 FREE Mystery Gifts.

Love Inspired® books feature contemporary inspirational romances with Christian characters facing the challenges of life and love.

FREE
Value Over
$20

YES! Please send me 2 FREE Love Inspired® Romance novels and my 2 FREE mystery gifts (gifts are worth about $10 retail). After receiving them, if I don't wish to receive any more books, I can return the shipping statement marked "cancel." If I don't cancel, I will receive 6 brand-new novels every month and be billed just $5.24 for the regular-print edition or $5.74 each for the larger-print edition in the U.S., or $5.74 each for the regular-print edition or $6.24 for the larger-print edition in Canada. That's a savings of at least 13% off the cover price. It's quite a bargain! Shipping and handling is just 50¢ per book in the U.S. and 75¢ per book in Canada.* I understand that accepting the 2 free books and gifts places me under no obligation to buy anything. I can always return a shipment and cancel at any time. The free books and gifts are mine to keep no matter what I decide.

Choose one: ☐ **Love Inspired® Romance Regular-Print**
(105/305 IDN GMY4)

☐ **Love Inspired® Romance Larger-Print**
(122/322 IDN GMY4)

Name (please print)

Address _____ Apt. #

City _____ State/Province _____ Zip/Postal Code

Mail to the **Reader Service:**
IN U.S.A.: P.O. Box 1341, Buffalo, NY 14240-8531
IN CANADA: P.O. Box 603, Fort Erie, Ontario L2A 5X3

Want to try 2 free books from another series! Call 1-800-873-8635 or visit www.ReaderService.com.

---

*Terms and prices subject to change without notice. Prices do not include sales taxes, which will be charged (if applicable) based on your state or country of residence. Canadian residents will be charged applicable taxes. Offer not valid in Quebec. This offer is limited to one order per household. Books received may not be as shown. Not valid for current subscribers to Love Inspired Romance books. All orders subject to approval. Credit or debit balances in a customer's account(s) may be offset by any other outstanding balance owed by or to the customer. Please allow 4 to 6 weeks for delivery. Offer available while quantities last.

Your Privacy—The Reader Service is committed to protecting your privacy. Our Privacy Policy is available online at www.ReaderService.com or upon request from the Reader Service. We make a portion of our mailing list available to reputable third parties that offer products we believe may interest you. If you prefer that we not exchange your name with third parties, or if you wish to clarify or modify your communication preferences, please visit us at www.ReaderService.com/consumerschoice or write to us at Reader Service Preference Service, P.O. Box 9062, Buffalo, NY 14240-9062. Include your complete name and address.

LI19R

"I wanted to talk to you about a project I'm getting started on. I'm opening a bakery."

"You are?" Annie couldn't keep the surprise out of her voice.

"Ja," Caleb said. "I stopped by to see if you'd be interested in working for me."

"You want to hire me? To work in your bakery?"

"I've had some success selling bread and baked goods at the farmers' market in Salem. Having a shop will allow me to sell year-round, but I can't be there every day and do my work at the farm. My sister Miriam told me you'd do a *gut* job for me."

"It sounds intriguing," Annie said. "What would you expect me to do?"

"Tend the shop and handle customers. There would be some light cleaning. I may need you to help with baking sometimes."

"Ja, I'd be interested in the job."

"Then it's yours. If you've got time now, I'll give you a tour of the bakery, and we can talk more about what I'd need you to do."

"*Gut.*" The wind buffeted her, almost knocking her from her feet.

She mumbled that she needed to let her twin, Leanna, know where she was going. He wrapped his arms around himself as another blast of wind struck them.

"Hurry…anna…" The wind swallowed the rest of his words as she rushed toward the house.

She halted midstep.

Anna?

Had Caleb thought he was talking to her twin? She'd clear everything up on their way to the bakery. She wanted the job. It was an answer to so many prayers, for God to let her find a way to help her sister be happy again, happy as Leanna had been before the man she loved married someone else without telling her.

Leanna was attracted to Caleb, and he'd be a fine match for her. Outgoing where her twin was quiet. A well-respected, handsome man whose *gut* looks would be the perfect foil for her twin's. But Leanna would be too shy to let Caleb know she was interested in him. That was where Annie could help.

As she was rushing to the house, she reminded herself of one vital thing. She must be careful not to let her own attraction to Caleb grow while they worked together.

That might be the hardest part of the job.

Don't miss
The Amish Bachelor's Baby *by Jo Ann Brown,*
available February 2019 wherever
Love Inspired® *books and ebooks are sold.*

www.LoveInspired.com

Looking for inspiration in tales
of hope, faith and heartfelt romance?

Check out **Love Inspired**® and
Love Inspired® **Suspense** books!

New books available every month!

CONNECT WITH US AT:

Facebook.com/groups/HarlequinConnection

 Facebook.com/HarlequinBooks

 Twitter.com/HarlequinBooks

 Instagram.com/HarlequinBooks

Pinterest.com/HarlequinBooks

ReaderService.com

Love Inspired®

LIGENRE2018R2